OBSTACLES

ODELIA CHAN

OBSTACLES

ONE GOD. ONE TEAM. ONE VISION.

Ambassador International
GREENVILLE, SOUTH CAROLINA & BELFAST, NORTHERN IRELAND

www.ambassador-international.com

Obstacles

ISBN: 978-1-64960-063-9
eISBN: 978-1-64960-068-4

Editing by Michelle Wyatt
Cover design by Hannah Linder Designs
Interior typesetting by Dentelle Design
Digital Edition by Anna Riebe Raats

Scripture taken from The King James Version. Public Domain.

AMBASSADOR INTERNATIONAL
Emerald House
411 University Ridge, Suite B14
Greenville, SC 29601, USA
www.ambassador-international.com

AMBASSADOR BOOKS
The Mount
2 Woodstock Link
Belfast, BT6 8DD, Northern Ireland, UK
www.ambassadormedia.co.uk

The colophon is a trademark of Ambassador, a Christian publishing company.

To My Family

PREFACE

DEAR READER,

It is my hope and prayer that you would be uplifted, encouraged, and inspired after reading this novel. God is able to use anything and everything for His glory and for His kingdom. Our job is to step out in faith and serve Him faithfully wherever He's placed us.

Parkour is a wonderful sport, and I would encourage you to explore it further after reading this book. There is a list of resources near the back of the book of books and videos I have found useful in both understanding and training Parkour and Freerunning: be sure to check out that list! Do realize, however, that Parkour is a dangerous sport and must be trained and practiced with patience and caution. Start small, stay safe, and train smart!

"For ye are bought with a price: therefore glorify God in your body, and in your spirit, which are God's." —1 Corinthians 6:20

In His Service,
Odelia Chan

ACKNOWLEDGMENTS

I THANK CHRIST JESUS, MY Lord and Savior, Who has given me this story to write and share with you. He is my only hope, my only fortress. May this book bring glory and praise to the one true God.

My heartfelt thanks to my wonderful family—all nine of them—for standing beside me. Mom and Dad, your support and prayers mean the world to me, and I could not have gone this far without both of you by my side. Thank you. I love you both. Tiffany, thank you for your ideas, critique, and encouragement: I could not have finished this book without your help and tireless spirit.

Thirdly, I would like to thank the wonderful people at Ambassador International who have worked so hard to bring this book to the world. Thank you so much for everything you've put into this project! You have made a dream come true.

I would like to thank all the freerunners and Parkour athletes who have inspired and guided me in my journey. Though too many to name, each of them has blessed my life in amazing ways that stretch far beyond the sport itself. Thank you from the bottom of my heart.

And finally, thank you, dear reader, for picking up this book and reading it. May it bless your heart and inspire your life to greater service for the King of Kings.

Live for Eternity!

PROLOGUE

THE SHARP PEBBLES LOOKED TREACHEROUS.

Leah reached up on tiptoes, brushed them off the top of the brick wall, then trotted back to the swing set a few yards to her left, where she'd planned to start her Parkour training for the day. She jumped toward the top bar holding up the two black plastic swings, felt the smooth, cool metal under her grip, then swung herself forward. Back and forth again. On the fourth swing, she lifted her knees and launched herself into a backward rotation, landing on her feet on the grass a second later. A perfect bar backflip. Next came the precision jumps—performed by leaping from one edge of an object to another. She sprinted to the nearest picnic table and began to practice her precisions, jumping from one side of the table to the edge of the seat of another.

Once she was satisfied with her jumps, she sprinted toward the brick wall she'd checked a few minutes ago. Here was the cherry-on-the-top for today's training session: a kong-gainer. She was familiar with the kong vault, which was a vault where one's legs pass under one's body, between one's two arms as the person vaults over an obstacle. Now she needed to combine the kong vault and a gainer—or a forward-moving backflip—and land on her feet on the other side of the wall.

This wall was easy—just the right height.

She jumped toward the wall, her arms reaching for the wall.

Her hands made contact with the top of the wall. She lifted her hips higher, tightening her torso as she brought her legs up underneath her. Once her legs cleared the top of the wall, she'd throw herself backward, tucking her knees to her chest in a backflip.

Then everything went wrong.

Her hands slipped off the top of the wall. She attempted to make up for the mistake, using her momentum to continue over the wall.

Her left leg moved a split second too slow. It did not clear the edge of the wall.

Sharp, excruciating pain radiated from Leah's left knee as her leg made contact with the unforgiving brick wall. Her knee loosened; pain forced her to freeze midair, and she fell to the ground, yelling out in pain, her knee twisted unnaturally beneath her.

I'll never do this again.

CHAPTER ONE

FIVE YEARS LATER . . .

Leah hesitated. The concrete slab six feet in front of her looked like an easy obstacle to vault over, but from her position on the edge of a huge flowerpot, she had no idea what lay beyond it.

There was one way to find out.

She balanced on the balls of her feet and tried to ignore the glares of passing strangers on the sidewalk parallel to the row of flowerpots behind the one she was on. She lifted her arms, jumping upwards and forwards, and landed in a perfect precision jump onto the three-inch-wide concrete slab.

She straightened from her crouched position, looked down, and found herself staring at an unbelievably handsome gentleman whose blue-grey eyes happened to glance upwards at the same moment.

Their eyes locked.

Leah straightened her athletic top, knowing that her hair was a lost cause. After the good hour she'd spent freerunning, her immaculate ponytail must look like a mess by now.

Not that she cared.

But compared with the immaculately dressed stranger making his way up the concrete staircase that led to the underground subway, her work-out clothes were a far cry from perfect. She scanned the man now sauntering towards her. He didn't look dangerous.

Leah switched back into her training mode. She looked up. The sun had moved since she'd last paid attention to it: it must be more than halfway through the afternoon now. She had more to go before she could log in her two hours of training Parkour.

"Need a hand down?" The devilish twinkle in those grey-blue eyes was unpredictable. Leah raised an eyebrow, shook her head, and hopped onto the ground.

He was now less than two feet away from her. Close enough for her to get a whiff of heady cologne. She swallowed her nausea and avoided his eyes, taking a careful step backward.

He was watching her. It was getting on her nerves. He looked familiar, but she could not, for the life of her, place where she'd seen him before.

For some strange reason, she felt an urge to flip. In front of him. For him? She knew better than that.

But it *was* her training session, and she'd only gone through training her underbars, precisions, and vaults. She had to nail down the double backflips and double front flips before she would call it a day.

She looked down at her scuffed shoes. The sole was peeling off near the tip. They would have to do for now.

The ground was perfect: dry and uncluttered.

She stepped forward, squatted, and threw a backflip, just to warm up.

The guy whistled. "That's a cool move you have there, miss . . . "

"Leah."

"Leah." He flashed a smile. "You have perfect form."

Leah kept her mouth shut, nodding in response. A good form was the result of persistent, consistent training—the only type of training worth her time.

She got into position for a double backflip—arms in front of her, bending into a squat like position, eyes looking straight ahead. Throwing her arms back, she powered through her knees, and felt herself rotating backward through the air. *One full rotation . . .*

Her ponytail whipped her in the face. She was moving a tad too slow. *One and a half rotation . . .*

"Marry me."

The second half of the second rotation never came. The jolt of surprise from the proposal—no, command—drained her body of all momentum, causing her to fall toward the ground in an inverted, curled position. Just when she was about to hit the ground face-on, strong arms wrapped around her torso and flipped her onto her feet.

Leah took a deep breath, her eyes closed to minimize the dizziness caused by the near crash. She looked up into a concerned face—and a pair of amused eyes. "Thanks. That was close. You . . . surprised me when you said . . . Nevermind."

"You're welcome, Leah." The easy grin was back on his face. His arms held onto her. She jostled them: he held on. She motioned with her hands, her eyes meeting his.

"Let me go."

"Why should I?" That grin was intolerable.

She turned sideways so that her shoulder touched his chest and jammed an elbow into his abdomen—not hard enough to hurt, but enough to loosen his grip on her waist.

She stepped back, shot the stranger a friendly yet annoyed glace—at least Leah hoped that was what it was—and walked away.

"You didn't even ask what my name was." He walked up to her from behind. Leah turned, eyes narrowed. His smile grew wider. "Is that how Asian girls are supposed to treat potential fiancés?"

Leah touched her wavy black hair. "Yeah. Especially those who make a joke of it."

"What gave it away? The glint of interest in my eyes?"

Goodness. She flashed him a tight smile. "It's not a proper proposal. So, of course, I would not dignify it with a proper response."

She turned to go. Hopefully, she could find a place where she could train without distractions.

"Hey." He stepped in front of her. "I'm just glad to find another freerunner."

Leah looked him over. He was bulkier than most men she'd trained with. But then, traceurs came in all shapes and sizes.

"You do Parkour?"

"I should say so." He scanned the surrounding area. Again, that profile. She must have seen this guy before.

"Are you training with anybody?" He turned back to her.

"Nope, all by my lonesome." Leah tossed the hair out of her face, her eyes sending him a challenge. He shrugged.

"You should know better than to freerun 'all by your lonesome.'" He made air quotations marks, teasing. He sobered. "Anything could happen. Think of what could have happened had I not been there to save you a few minutes ago."

The botched kong-gainer of two years ago surfaced in her memories, bringing pain, bitterness, defeat. Her hands fisted, her mind refusing to relive the past. She forced herself to relax. "If you hadn't opened your mouth the way you did at the time you did, I could have finished standing up. But thanks for saving me all the same."

"Your appreciation is appreciated." He bowed, eyes twinkling. "Still, find yourself a group to train with."

"What does it matter to you?" Her watch beeped. Time to get back into the real world.

"I'm just doing what I can to keep one more beautiful face on the earth." His voice was surprisingly soft. And smooth. And familiar.

Leah pressed her lips together, turning to face him squarely. "Thanks so much for your concern, sir . . . I still don't know what your name is. I'm starting to wonder if you have one." She tried to cover the sarcasm in her voice with a smile.

"Maybe you could train with me sometime?"

"That an invitation?"

"Yes." He looked at her. His eyes were sincere yet still playful. "I've been part of a team that does Parkour for a living. Teaching, speaking, putting on shows, things like that. I'd like to start my own—along with a privately-owned gym. You could be part of it." He raised his eyebrows.

"A Parkour group sounds great. Maybe I'll start one of my own someday," she grinned at him.

She was surprised at the fierce, hard look that passed over his face at the mention of her creating her own group—a glare that was quickly replaced with a friendly smile.

"Glad to be an inspiration." His words lacked conviction and warmth.

He turned to walk away. Seeing she had nothing to lose, Leah called out a farewell.

"Promise me you'll take care of yourself." He half-turned, eyes drilling into hers over his shoulder.

"I always do." Leah smiled.

He shrugged, then made as if to walk away.

Her mind snapped into action: a Parkour group, a chiseled face, blond hair, and striking blue eyes.

Yes, she'd definitely seen this guy before. But never in person. She took a second look. There was a Parkour group she'd caught wind of when she started training herself.

They called themselves Team Lightning. They were known as one of the leading freerunning groups in the area. They'd been her inspiration. A team member had decided to leave the team and pursue his own ambitions a few months ago. He had blond hair, blue eyes that smoked through the camera, a muscular form, and strong cheekbones.

The reality struck her.

The man turned to her for one lingering second. "Name's Ethan Simpson. I'll see you around."

Speechless, Leah watched him saunter away.

CHAPTER TWO

The cream Subaru had been tailing her Jeep for the past five minutes. Leah glanced at the rearview mirror, trying to identify the driver inside the Subaru. The windshield was just too reflective. The sun was gone, but the rain splashing onto both cars' windows disrupted her vision. She made out the figure of a man. Something about that determined chin jogged her memory.

She mentally ran through the people she'd met recently. That was it. Ethan. It had been only two days since the interrupted training session. What was he doing here?

Shrugging, Leah put the disturbing thought out of her mind and turned into the nearest parking lot.

She steered her burgundy Jeep into an empty spot and killed the engine. The green and yellow Panera Bread sign smiled down from her on her left. Leah snatched up her purse and stepped out of the car. The cream Subaru was nowhere to be seen. Still, knowing it was around unsettled her.

She scanned the parking lot for anything that seemed out of place. Nothing looked strange, except that the parking lot seemed rather empty for a Saturday morning. All the better for a quiet morning with a honey-sweetened latte and maybe a gluten-free pastry—if they offered dietary choices.

She pulled open the door, inhaling the aroma of freshly baked bread that greeted her. She scanned the tables. Most of the seats were empty. Torontonians were not exactly early risers, especially on an overcast Saturday morning.

Leah headed to a corner booth where she could gaze out onto the street yet still be deep enough in the shadows to not attract attention. She sat down, scanned the few cars in the parking lot again, and breathed a sigh of relief. No cream Subaru was in sight.

A girl cleaned the table next to hers. She looked familiar. Black hair pulled back into a long braid. Golden skin tones. The girl turned to give her a welcoming smile.

"Shana? That you?" Leah dropped her purse on the seat beside her, rising to give the girl a hug.

Two lean arms wrapped around her briefly. Shana stepped back. "Yeah, it's me, Leah." The grin on her face was infectious, and Leah felt her own lips curling into a smile.

"How long has it been? Two years? Three?" Leah maneuvered to her seat, taking off her damp jacket and laying it beside her purse. "When did you start working here?"

"A few months ago." Shana balanced a cleaning spray bottle and mop in her left hand, gesturing with her right. "I don't think we've gotten together for three years now . . . the last time I saw you was at that summer camp. You were around eighteen years old then, I believe?"

"I'm twenty now. That would make it two years. A long time."

"Too long," Shana nodded.

An awkward pause ensued. Sleepy-looking patrons shuffled in, their gazes landing on them for uninterested split-seconds. Leah turned back to Shana.

"Catch me up. What have you been up to since we moved away?"

Shana hesitated. "Let me ask a co-worker to take over for a few minutes." She winked at Leah and hurried away.

Leah sat down and reached for the menu lying on the center of the table. She scanned for gluten-free options. No luck. She flipped the booklet over to the drinks section. No sugar-free, lactose-free option here—unless she ordered black coffee with nothing else. She definitely did not drive over here to drink bitter dirt water.

"Ready to order?" Shana materialized beside her, a professional smile on her face. "Oh—my apologies. You won't find any gluten-free, sugar-free dairy-free options there." The caramel eyes twinkled.

"You still remember?" Leah smiled back.

"I should! Remember we brought food to your family each week when your mother was ill the last year you lived next to us? When you said your mom couldn't eat store-bought bread, my cousin learned to make gluten-free bread and noodles and brought them to her instead." Shana held her head a little higher. "He's such an amazing cook . . . "

Shana's cousin. Victor Menchaca. The dark-haired boy who'd lighted up her family's days in the city while her mother battled cancer. Maybe she even fell in love with him during those teenage years. Leah's father had decided to move back to the country after mother's chemo treatments were over, and she had to leave her dearest friends behind. Her mother soon recovered, but she'd lost contact with Vic and couldn't thank him for all he'd done for them, for her. She could still hear his laughter, see his eyes twinkle.

Leah blinked the memories away. For all she knew, Vic was married or had a girlfriend already. Two years can change so much. She had no right to think such thoughts, anyways . . .

Leah realized Shana was staring at her expectantly. "Sorry, what did you say?"

Shana grinned, lowering herself onto the chair opposite Leah. "Get that dreamy look off your face. I was asking you about your family, but then you completely zoned out."

Leah touched her cheeks with the back of her fingers. Not hot, thankfully. But they were getting warmer under Shana's knowing look. "My family's doing great. And I did not have a dreamy look on my face. It's just been a while since I've seen y'all."

"Glad to hear. And . . . you're probably dying to know what Vic's up to now."

Leah's head jerked up, despite herself.

"Ha. Gotcha." Shana smirked and forged on. "He's majoring in computer engineering and plans to graduate within the year. He already has jobs lined up around the area." Shana fingered the glass of water in her hands, her eyes wandering around the restaurant. "Relationship wise . . . " She paused as if savoring the suspense. Leah drew in a breath and held it. "Still single. And you?"

"Yeah, still single." Leah exhaled. Better change the subject now. "So, what about you? You're finished with high school. What's the plan?"

Shana smiled. "Remember that online college study platform you introduced me to? I've been working on my Bachelor's in Education, minoring in math."

"That's nice. Math teacher, huh?" Shana nodded, avoiding Leah's eyes. "Good for you. How much longer to go?"

"I'm taking a gap year. I have to get the money to pay for my last two years' of tuition."

"Halfway done. Good news. Is the work good here?" Leah waved her hand, gesturing at the counter where another waitress stood.

Shana shrugged. "It's good, I guess. I have friends here, so that's a bonus." She turned to Leah. "What about you?"

"I skipped college and took a couple of courses on bookkeeping instead. I've been working as a virtual assistant and freelance writer."

"Lots of free time then?"

"Depends on the day, but mostly yes. I'm my own boss." Leah laughed at the jealous expression on Shana's face. "I do stay busy, though."

"Doing what?"

"Parkour. I train whenever and wherever I could."

"Parkour." Shana mused. "You told me you were interested in that crazy sport years ago. You're still onto it?"

"I've been doing Parkour for four years now. I've had only a knee injury, a couple of bruises and scrapes so far. You?"

"I don't freerun the way you do. My cousin and Guy—his best buddy, you remember?" Leah nodded. "They both do Parkour every chance they get. I see it as an adrenaline junkie thing, not . . . whatever you traceurs think it is." She waved a hand dismissively.

"Join me next week. I'll give you a call if you want to get together after your shift and watch me free-run. Maybe I'll be able to convince you."

"Fat chance." Shana snickered. She took a notebook from her apron, scribbled down her number and email address, and tore the sheet off, handing it to Leah.

"Here you go. Random question, but how do you glorify God with Parkour?"

Leah had her model answer ready. "It's a way to glorify God with the body and strength He has given me. Praising Him through movement." But as she said it, it felt lacking, incomplete, unsatisfying.

Leah tried to shake off the feeling. She looked at the scrap of paper in her hand.

Shana's email address was still the same. Somehow, they'd drifted apart even after being in close contact for a few years. "Some things never change, eh?" Leah noted as she folded the paper and stuck it in her purse.

"Like how you feel about my cousin? Has that ever changed? I faintly remember all those years ago, the afternoon visits, the way you looked at him when you thought no one else was looking . . . "

"Stop." Shana was right—too much so. But Leah was only a young teen then. Still, Vic had already captured her heart and held it for all those years. And now? "Keep those memories to yourself." Leah paused, hating how hard and hurt her voice sounded. She softened her tone. "It's in the past, Shana. We were just friends. He was kind to my sisters and me. Nothing more."

"There are second chances in life sometimes." Shana smiled softly, her eyes holding onto Leah's. "I guess you'll never know until you see him again."

"I've got to go, Shana." Leah nodded at Shana's raised eyebrows. "Yes, I work Saturdays, too. I pay for that with half-days off all week." Leah grinned and picked up her purse and jacket. "I'll give you a call when I train again. It was nice seeing you again."

"I'll be waiting for your call. Surprise me." One last smirk from Shana, a wave, and Leah turned away, making her way against the flow of patrons coming into the restaurant. She paused on the sidewalk, looked around, and walked to her Jeep.

The head of a cream Subaru peeked from just behind the far side of the retail building in front of her as she stepped into her car. Leah blinked, and the car came to life and disappeared around the corner.

CHAPTER THREE

"Any additional thoughts on this passage?" The salt-and-pepper-haired gentleman at the end of the table spoke, his hand on the open Bible in front of him.

Leah shook her head, along with the other young people in the room.

"It was a good message, pastor." The blond-haired young man seated next to her affirmed. "Daniel was certainly a great example of dedication, loyalty, and courage in living out one's faith."

Sam's words brought someone to Leah's mind. Javin. And Javin's brother. She remembered meeting Javin's brother, Trevor, noticing the closeness between the two brothers. Only after their friendship—Leah's and Javin's—had deepened had she dared to ask Javin about his past: a dark and sorrowful story that had left her in tears.

Long story short, Trevor led Javin to the Lord and encouraged him to walk on the straight and narrow path through all of life's difficulties. Trevor was an example to Javin—and herself—of how selfless and courageous a Christian should live: bold, fearless, and unashamed in Christ.

She wondered where Javin was. They'd first met the year before last, at a summer camp. He was a volunteer, she was part of the staff, which made her a boss of sorts over him—a fact he took pleasure in pointing out every so often. The summer ended, and they went back to their separate lives, barely keeping in touch.

Then they'd met unexpectedly last year. They were catching up with each other's lives when he said something she disagreed with. She shot back a hurtful remark, and what was at first a friendly chat became a heated discussion. Leah's face burned as she remembered how furious she'd felt, how sarcastic her replies were.

The subject was of no significance now, but she still remembered it.

It was about apples, of all things.

She focused on the present and nodded at Sam. "I agree. That's a good point."

"Very well. You all are welcome to leave. Thank you for coming to study the Word with us." Pastor Michael beamed, rising.

An assorted chorus of "See you Pastor! Thank you, sir!" filed past through the door.

Leah lingered behind.

"May I ask you a question, Pastor Michael?" Leah fiddled with her purse strings, keeping an eye on her pastor. She could trust him to give her a straight answer.

"Sure go ahead, Leah. I'm not disappearing anytime soon." He chuckled, settling back into his chair. "What's on your mind?"

Leah hesitated. Since the chance meeting with Ethan, her mind had been spinning with the possibility of starting a Parkour group in the area—a group of Christian people, young or old, to build up and edify each other through training.

Still, that sense of incompleteness lingered. Helping each other was not enough. There had to be something more. Something that could bring light into the community.

"Pastor . . . what are teens in this day and age most in need of, besides knowledge of the gospel and trust in the Lord?"

Pastor Michael rubbed his chin. "That's a good question. You're barely out of the teen years yourself."

"I'm twenty, sir." Leah shot back, smiling. "I have an idea, and I'm wondering if it would do any good in helping teens in the area."

"I like that you're thinking deeply about your own generation: you're on the right track. Hmmm . . . besides Christ? There's nothing you need." He grinned at her. "I get the idea, but always make sure that Christ is center and foremost in whatever work you do."

"Of course, sir. There is more, though."

"I definitely agree, Leah. I'll say that teenagers today are lacking personal responsibility. They expect everything to be done for them and to reap the benefits themselves."

Leah dug out a notebook and pen. "Let me write that down." *Personal responsibility.*

"They need to know that everything they do—everything they say has consequences. Every act is the result of an idea, and ideas have consequences. They should know what those consequences are, and why.

"Another significant point is having a vision. A mission in life. They have to know that they're part of something bigger than themselves. They are important pieces in a mega puzzle God is putting together for this world."

A vision, or meaning in life. Part of a bigger picture, went onto Leah's purple notepad.

"On top of those two big points—and besides all the almost clichés ideas such as having good friends, not wasting time on their phones, etcetera, etcetera—I'll say that these young people need good mentors. Preferably godly Christian ones. They need people who would challenge them, encourage them, and show them what it means to live redeemed lives."

"That makes sense, sir." Leah scribbled down *good mentors.* "Thank you for your thoughts."

"Thank you. I love knowing that young people are standing up to meet the big lions in our culture. I'll be praying as you seek the answers and conclusion to whatever ideas you have going on in that head of yours."

"Thanks. Good day, sir."

CHAPTER FOUR

Leah ran her fingers over the sole of the black runner. The rubber felt strong. The body of the shoe was made of breathable material, and it was a stretchy, slip-on shoe—no strings attached. Perfect for freerunners who'd rather not trip over a wayward shoestring.

Leah turned the shoe over and cheeked for size. A women's size eight. She smiled to herself, picked up the pair, and headed over to the bench a few paces off, where a man was trying on different pairs of running shoes.

"Mind if I take a seat?" Leah asked with a smile, adjusting her bag and preparing to sit down.

The man shifted and smiled up at her. One look into those inviting blue eyes and she was ready to turn tail and run to the other bench.

She shot a glance that way. A lean, long-legged guy crouched over his freerunners. She studied him for a couple of seconds. Brownish skin tone, angular face half hidden under the hood. Had she met that guy before?

She was trying too hard to come up with an excuse to move away from Ethan Simpson.

She looked at his grinning face. Day-old stubble made him look hotter, if that was even possible. It annoyed her.

"I don't mind you sitting beside me, here or anywhere, now or for all time."

Leah ignored his flirtatious glance. "Thanks." She sat down and did what she had to do: try on her shoes and make a decision. Her income was not all that decadent, so each dollar had to count.

"Those runners look cute on you."

"Thank you," she muttered, willing a blush to stay away.

They tried on their respective shoes in silence. Leah got up, sprinting down empty aisles and doing jumps in the air to make sure the shoes were a good fit. Nope: they didn't provide enough space for her toes to spread out and find a grip. But the price was affordable.

She shook her head and stood.

"They don't work for you?" Ethan quirked an eyebrow at her, picking up his two pairs of running shoes and standing beside her. The top of her head came only to his neck. Leah arched her neck to look at him.

"I'll have to think about it." She moved to get her bag lying a foot away from Ethan.

A hand grabbed her wrist.

"Let me go." Leah flicked her wrist in a circular motion, snatched her hand away before he could tighten his grip, and grabbed her purse.

"Had a bad day at work?"

Her tone had been testy. He deserved that. But he was still a person made in God's image and should be treated as such. She took a deep breath. "No. I'm just . . . looking for the perfect shoe."

"Here, I'll look with you. Help you out. Trust me?"

"Got experience, huh?" Leah gave him a smile she hoped wasn't too strained. "I'm good, thanks." She stepped toward the display case where she'd picked up the pair she'd just tried on.

Footsteps sounded behind her. They paused close by. A little too close.

She whirled around. Her ponytail whipped whoever it was behind her in the face.

Ethan brushed a hand down his face. "That was uncalled for."

"Stop following me around."

The sparkle in his eyes reminded her of a totally different spark, also from those same eyes: hatred, deep and dangerous. She looked away. "I'm good, Ethan. You can go do your own stuff." She waved at the hundreds of shoes on the shelves, essentially waving him away.

"I am doing my own stuff." He murmured, stepping even closer. She moved a step away, glancing at the exit door out of the corner of her eyes. If things ever got out of hand, there's the clip-on Gerber knife at her hip, her self-defense skills, and the exit door.

"You can't stop me from following my dreams." He tilted his head and grinned.

"I thought your dream was to create your own Parkour group after leaving Team Lightning?" She quirked an eyebrow at him.

"Ah. So you do know who I am," he smirked, leaning against the wall beside the shoe displays. "Well, I have more dreams than just the one."

"Stop thinking of me as one of them."

"I can't stop since I saw you attempt to do the double flip." That condescending smirk was too much.

She tilted her head at him. "Thanks again for saving me. I'll go and try these on now. Catch you later."

Leah snatched up a perfect-looking pair of shoes totally beyond her budget. She fast-walked to the nearest bench, watching Ethan sulk his way to the men's section, which happened to be quite a distance from the bench he occupied before.

She sighed, sat down, removed the flats she'd worn over to this place, and slipped on the shoes she'd just picked out: black with hints of purple, and no strings. She checked the sole—no hard, slick plastic, all flexible and rubbery, with good friction. She shot a glance at the price tag and sighed.

"You freerun?"

The voice was unmistakable. The last time she'd heard it, it was just starting to break, but it was still the same husky voice. Her eyes traveled up a pair of new shoes, black exercise pants, and a tank top, stopping at two intelligent eyes that peered into hers.

One look from Guy gave her the impression that her entire soul was bare. As if he could see every corner of her being. He'd stare at a person, his eyes unwavering, calm, probing.

That was the stare he was giving her now.

Taken by surprise, it took her a moment to answer his question. "Yes, I do. I'm assuming you do, too?"

"Yeah." A dry chuckle. "After Vic dared me to try it out. I was hooked on the fourth day of training."

Leah smiled. "What went wrong the first few days?"

"The normal scrapes and bruises, I guess. Nothing major, but they weren't minor either—at least not to me." He shifted his weight from one foot to another, finally lowering himself beside her, keeping a respectful distance. Leah appreciated that.

They sat in silence, lost in their own thoughts. Guy had left her life along with Vic and Shana. Guy and Vic were as close as brothers—the only brother either ever had.

"Where do you work?" Guy turned toward her, toeing off the new shoes and bending to put on his old ones.

"From home."

Guy nodded, looking up from his bent position. "Same here. What do you do?"

"I help businesses and companies sort out their paperwork, answer their customers' questions and requests, solve logistical issues, schedule and reschedule stuff, those kinds of things." She slipped on the new shoes. "I write articles, stories, blog posts, and e-books on the side."

Guy nodded again. "And?"

"That's about it. Mom said I either had to get a job or get married, so I went with the former. It seems safer and more predictable."

There was an awkward silence, then Guy laughed. Something Leah never heard from him. A free, uninhibited laugh.

She couldn't help but smile with him. "What's so funny? Is my makeup all smeared up?"

"What? You wore makeup? For him?" He stuck a thumb in the direction Ethan had gone.

Face aflame, Leah turned to check if the man in question was within hearing distance. He was. And by the smug, satisfied look on his face, he'd heard that last bit.

"Since when did you start using makeup? I thought you homeschoolers *never* did." Guy's incredulous voice broke through her embarrassment.

"Stop stereotyping country-raised homeschoolers. That's not true. And that's not nice, either." Leah propped her chin on a fist and stared him down. "And I definitely would not do myself up for him."

"Hardly convinced. You guys were flirting up a storm." Guy grunted, his eyes challenging hers.

"Sure. I haven't been returning his attention." She shrugged and slipped on the other shoe.

"You never tried to make yourself pretty for Vic, did you?"

His voice was quiet, but the question sent shockwaves through her. She whirled in her seat to face Guy.

"That's out of line, Guy," she said in a whisper. "It was nothing but a teenage crush. Vic never noticed me. And to answer your question, I did do everything I could to make myself cute for him, short of doing anything inappropriate." Leah shot a glance at him. Somehow, she knew she could trust him with this part of her past.

Guy skipped a beat. He looked at her. "He never knew. I suppose you never knew how hard he fell for you all those years ago, eh?"

"You got to be in the middle of it all—you and Shana. Knowing both sides of the story, which was more than Vic and I got." She stopped herself and gave Guy a wry smile.

They both focused back on the tasks at hand. The shoes felt too good to be real. She gave the shoes the sprinting and jumping test, then returned to the bench, smiling.

Guy watched her, eyes contemplative. "Good ones?"

"Yeah." Leah lovingly placed the shoes beside her on the bench and pulled on her flats once more. "Too pricey, though." She gathered up the shoes. "You haven't told me what you were up to yet. You once said you wanted to go into tech—coding, programming, and stuff. How is that working out?"

"Pretty well." Guy paused. "I'm part of a software company that offers various computer services. I'm their white hat guy. I love hacking gigs."

"Fighting the bad guys with logic and technology, eh?"

"Exactly. Totally enjoyable." They stood and walked over to the counter together. On the way, Leah replaced the perfect shoes with a sigh, then grabbed the first pair she'd tried on and caught up with Guy.

"You had a knee injury years ago?"

"Shana told you?"

Guy nodded, his eyes concerned. "She didn't know why, though. What happened?"

Leah tensed at the memory. She couldn't let herself go back there. "Don't worry. That was years ago. I'll be okay." She shook her head to clear her thoughts, smiling at Guy.

"You need someone to take care of you." Guy shook his head, muttering. He swiped his card—debit, Leah noticed, just like her—and took up his shoebox with one hand. He turned to her. "There's no one I know who could do that better than Vic." He took a step back, locked eyes with her for a few seconds, and then lifted his hand in a silent wave.

He turned to go.

Someone opened the front door. Someone who'd grown up some since the last time she'd seen him. Someone with curly dark hair and an amazing smile.

The newcomer turned to her as Guy said something. Their eyes locked in a long stare. Her face flushed with warmth, and she looked at the ground, her hands tightening on the bag in her hands to keep herself from running to him.

She composed herself and looked up. He was still there, but he didn't seem inclined to talk to her. He just smiled. And for some reason, that disappointed her. But it had been so long since they'd last seen each other anyways. They were not kids anymore. Perhaps the past, with all its heartbreaks and memories, was best left alone.

Guy lifted a hand and waved. Leah waved back. Her eyes sought Vic's of their own accord. Then both of them turned to go.

Leah stood feeling strangely bereft and alone, watching two of her dearest childhood friends walk out the front door of the shoe shop and into the busy street beyond.

The cashier's voice broke into her reverie, and she paid for her shoes.

CHAPTER FIVE

LATER THAT WEEK . . .

The last invoice was accounted for. Leah clicked open different account pages, scrolled through them to check her work, then closed all the tabs and shut off the computer. She tidied up her front desk, picked up her purse in the foyer, and locked the apartment door behind her.

Her dream car sat all alone in the empty parking lot. A burgundy Jeep. A gas-guzzling creature that had been her graduation gift from her grandparents. Minimizing her driving brought the sum total of expense to just affordable.

She pulled out of the parking lot, one hand on the steering wheel, buckling herself in with the other. The parking lot was tiny compared to the ones in the sprawling complexes in the suburbs where she'd grown up, but this was downtown Toronto, where parking spots were a treasured, and expensive, rarity.

She turned into the slow-moving traffic, carefully making her way through the crowded streets. Cars honked here and there. People walked along the sidewalks. Bikers and joggers went past her, trying to get in their daily quota of exercise after work.

She studied the road before her. Suddenly, from her peripheral vision, a young man darted out into the street, throwing himself on the ground between her moving Jeep and the Mercedes in front of her.

Leah slammed on the brakes. The car behind her blew its horn, but she did not care.

Leah snapped on her hazard lights, placed the car in *park*—there was nowhere for her to pull to the side, trapped as she was between the man on the ground in front of her and the car very close behind her—and jumped out of the car.

"Sir? Are you okay?" Leah crouched at the prone figure lying a few inches from her Jeep's front tires. No blood, thank God. But also—no sound. She tapped the hunched shoulders. Did he faint?

"Is he okay? Tell me he's okay!!" A hysterical woman's voice came from the sidewalk. A fortyish woman, in slacks and a T-shirt, ran toward her. She clutched at her hands, her face expressing inner turmoil.

"He is breathing." Leah motioned to the young man. On hearing the sound of the woman's voice, the young man looked up at Leah and shook his head. "You should not have stopped the car. I wanted this all to be over." He pulled himself up with a grimace, then staggered to his feet.

Leah stared at the hard, bitter face of the young man who looked just a few years younger than herself. What could have driven him to do such a rash thing?

"We just visited the doctor." The woman placed her arms around the young man, gripping him to herself. "He told us Paul would not be able to train to be a triathlon ever again. That drove him to the edge."

Leah nodded.

"Was at the top of my age group the past competition. One accident was all it took to crush those dreams." Paul looked back at Leah, his eyes devoid of emotion, of life.

"He was biking on the road when a guy in front of him opened the driver's side door. He blew his bike horn. The guy popped back into his car but did not bother to close the door after himself." The mother shook her head.

"I was training for speed. I could not stop in time. Crashed straight into that open door. The impact threw me off the bike and onto the roof of another car who had stopped at the intersection a little ways ahead." Paul looked at the ground. "By that time, my back and head were throbbing in pain. But that was nothing compared to what the asphalt did to me as I slid off the car roof, bumped past the sedan's trunk, and crashed onto the street."

"Wow. You're blessed to still be alive." Leah held out a hand. "You're a strong person for surviving that."

"No broken bones. I got through junior high on painkillers and a ton of physio work. But the doc said I'll never compete again. Not in the sport that was my life." He looked away, tears filling his blue eyes.

"I'm eternally grateful to you for saving my son's life." The woman reached out a hand to grip Leah's. "He's all I have." Tears ran down the woman's cheek. Leah's eyes filled with sympathetic tears.

"Thank God he's safe."

Paul moved as if to leave. His mother laid a hand on his arm. "Paul and I would love to see you again; get to know you better. But it seems like the city of Toronto is getting mad at you." The woman pointed, a tremulous smile on her lips.

Leah turned. It did seem like her Jeep was garnering a generous amount of negative reactions.

She turned to the mother and son. "I'd love to stay in touch." She reached into her pocket, scribbled her email address onto a sheet of paper, then handed it to the woman. "I'll be praying for both of you. Paul, I hope you feel better soon."

She gave them a smile, waved, and stepped back toward her Jeep.

Once inside, she turned back toward the sidewalk and watched the mother reach up to wrap her arm around Paul's shoulder. He said something to her, then slowly, painfully, they made their way down the sidewalk.

Was there something she could do to help people like Paul, who were trapped behind broken dreams, broken pasts, broken hearts?

CHAPTER SIX

The weather was too inviting. She would train outdoors instead.

Leaving the Vault's parking lot, Leah made her way down the street toward the park she usually trained in, nodding to hurried-looking men and women rushing past. Most of the park's structures and surrounding areas were empty: a few young mothers and their babies played in the tiny tot's playground. Things were good as long as no one got hurt. She was not planning to do that today.

Leah placed her lunch bag onto a wooden bench and picked up her phone. She reached into her purse, dug out Shana's phone number, and typed it in. She held the phone to her ear, closing her eyes briefly and taking a deep breath of city air. She missed the clear country air even a cool Canadian April noon in Toronto could not give her.

Three rings. Then, voice message.

She switched to texting and gave Shana the location she was about to train in. Leah added a smiley face and told her to bring her lunch with her: they would chat over a picnic lunch and Parkour.

Shana's navy sedan rolled up to the curb a few minutes later. Shana gracefully stepped out of the car, looked around, and spied Leah. Her face broke into a wide smile. She leaned back into her car to take out her purse and a sizable cooler bag, then locked her car and trotted over.

"You monkey around here?"

"Anywhere." Leah tried to see the random plastic and concrete structures scattered throughout the park through Shana's eyes. There were spots where she could practice cat leaps and rail precisions—anything, really—thanks to the big kids-sized playground neatly situated in the middle.

Even the benches and picnic tables were top quality freerunning tools. Overcoming obstacles—any kind, all of them—was the name of the game.

Shana stepped up to a wooden bench, laid down a chic-looking cooler bag, and brushed her hair from her face, tying it into a bun. Then she went straight into a full-blown stretching session.

Shana turned her attention back on Leah, coming back to an upright position after touching her toes for a hamstring stretch. "What?"

"I thought you were just going to munch your lunch and watch me try to kill myself." Leah grinned.

Shana brought her right elbow behind her head, pulling it to the left with her other hand. "I don't get why you go outdoors to train while the Vault is just down the street? Why deal with all the elements if you have a gym and all the amenities that affords?"

Leah thought for a moment. "I think I would have to give you a short lecture on the sport itself before I could convince you to think my way, or at least understand where I'm coming from."

"I'm all ears." Shana sat on the bench patting the seat beside her. "We are eating lunch first then?"

"Sure." Leah sat down, took out her sandwich, and glanced over at Shana. "Would you like to pray for this meal?"

"Sure." Shana shrugged, closed her eyes, and bowed her head. Leah closed her eyes.

"Dear God, thank You for this sunny day. Bless the food we are about to eat, help me to stay awake while Leah lectures me on Parkour, and keep us—Leah mostly—safe while she demonstrates freerunning to this beginner. In Jesus' name, amen."

"Amen." Leah grinned at the playful jabs in the prayer and lifted the sandwich to her mouth. Shana's voice made her pause.

"That's gluten-free?" Skepticism colored her tone.

"Yep, not a speck of gluten. I made it, so I should know." Leah took a bite, sighing with happiness. It tasted just as good as she hoped.

"Hmm. Guess my cousin would have a hard time convincing you to eat what you'll call junk food, if what you eat looks that good already. I brought pastries from Panera."

"Smells great." Leah stared at the assortment of bite-sized baked goods. "Looks nice."

"Yeah. The perks of working at a restaurant without having dietary restrictions." Shana took a bite, glanced over, and shielded her full mouth while muttering, "No offense, Leah."

"None taken." They focused on their respective lunches for a while.

Shana cleared her throat. "So tell me about Parkour. What it is, how it came to be, and how and why you became so passionate about it."

"What gave?"

Shana emitted a short laugh. "Your face shines each time Parkour comes up in a conversation. Dreamy, happy, excited, hopeful . . . I'm running out of adjectives."

Leah nodded. "Yes. I *am* passionate."

"And?" Shana looked at her expectantly.

"All right. Prepare for a long-winded overview of the stuntman's secret obsession."

"That's really what it is?" Shana quirked an eyebrow.

"It's a lot more than just that, but yes, Parkour can be found in stunt acting moves. It's considered an extreme sport by many since practitioners and freerunners throw themselves into many seemingly dangerous moves and jumps. Hopefully, what I will say will take away some of that negativity I can see on your skeptical face."

Shana grinned. "Remember: I've got a cousin and friend who's just as crazy about this thing as you are. It's not all that new to me."

"Good. But to many, Parkour is a sport that seems only to feed the thirst for adrenaline in young people. But really, it was born out of watching how people naturally overcome obstacles in their own way. Notice how kids jump, roll, and swing themselves when having fun in playgrounds?" Shana nodded. "That's basically what we're doing. We're having fun with the environment. It just looks more dangerous because we're a couple of sizes bigger than kids.

"But—back to its roots. During the First World War, Georges Herbert, a French naval officer, created an army obstacle course for training. He took aspects of human movement he observed natives using while scrambling away from natural disasters threatening their lives. Faced with a life or death situation, you'd overcome any obstacle to stay alive, right? He noted that there were a couple of movements basic to his Parkour training—jumping, running, swimming, and climbing—so on, so forth.

"A guy named Raymond Belle participated in these classes. He grew to love the idea, later developing his own version of non-combatant Parkour, a training and mindset—a belief, really—that he passed on to his son, David Belle, whom many today consider the father of Parkour.

"As David grew up, he kept pushing himself to the limit to do his best. Through his efforts, this sport was refined and professionalized. David was part of a group of young people: a group that had a huge impact on the direction Parkour was to take in the pages of history. They were the Yamasaki."

"I remember watching the movie with Vic." Shana nodded for her to go on.

"Of course, reality was tougher than the sensationalized film, but the idea was the same. From that small group of young people came what is known today as Parkour and freerunning. Some say that there's no line between the two. The way I understand it, however, is that the mindset or approach to these two physical disciplines is different. The moves might look similar, but the goal pursued in either is different. In Parkour, the goal is to overcome all obstacles using only the body and mind. This means getting over, under, or around things that stand in one's way when reaching a destination."

"Which would mean a focus on moves like vaults, precision jumps, running, bounding, and the like?"

"Exactly. Freerunning focuses more on the aesthetic or creative side of movement in that it encourages one to interact more creatively and joyfully with the environment, as opposed to a mainly overcoming viewpoint."

"Which would mean doing flips in mid-air, things like that?"

"Yes. Corks, Kong gainers—things that shy away from the one focus of getting past obstacles and reaching a finish point."

"By your definition, many people who say they practice Parkour are really just freerunning, or they've mixed things up." Shana raised her eyebrows.

"Uh-huh. I like to say I'm a traceur, but to be honest, most of the time I'm freerunning. I do Parkour—I know how, and at times I specifically train that—but when you see me flipping and spinning around, yes, that's creative freerunning."

"So, why this sport? Why not, soccer, basketball, or anything else?"

"Basketball? Ha! That was my first love." Leah grimaced. "Never grew tall enough to play competitively. Sure, I could shoot hoops now and then, but I'll mostly be the gal in the back passing balls. And for that—too much pressure, not enough fun." Leah shrugged. "I like soccer, but I don't run fast enough to be good enough for people to want me to be on their team. The ball tends to shy away from me when I try to make contact with it, know what I mean?"

Shana lifted a shoulder. "Why not other independent sports, at least ones that don't involve team pressure?"

"Badminton and the like? I do enjoy them, but somehow I just can't find the passion or motivation to practice, train, and actually be very good at things with a racket."

"That leaves you with this and track,"

"Again, I love to run, but I'm not the best sprinter. So I thought, why not freerun?"

"How did you know about this anyway?" Shana tilted her head, biting into a chocolate croissant.

"How can you eat that and stay so fit?" Leah faked a whiny voice and grinned.

"You're not out of shape yourself. You've got no reason to complain." Shana threw back.

"Whatever." Leah smiled. "What was I saying? Oh yes. I fell in love with this sport after watching a couple of YouTube videos. I know."

Leah noted, noticing Shana's climbing eyebrows. "I discovered this team of traceurs who took my breath away with their performances, and they've been my inspiration ever since." A picture of Ethan flashed through her mind, temporarily clouding the bright memories. "Then I got into training in my own backyard and basement. I finished high school, moved back to the city, started working, and have been practicing all that I can both here and at the Vault."

"The gym down the road from here?" Shana asked. Leah nodded.

Shana continued, "I suppose you practiced your vaults over pasture fences and gates in the country?"

"Yeah. Living on a hobby farm had its pros and cons—there was the added motivation for not falling, since landing in a pile of manure was—so not nice."

Shana made a face. "I could imagine."

Leah finished her sandwich, took a bite of her cookie, and got up. "Without further ado, let's get into the action."

Shana bundled up the wax paper that held her pastries, stuck it in the cooler bag, and drew out two cartons of yogurt. "Get the show on." She dug into the vanilla and strawberry mix with a spoon. "Show me. When I'm finished, I just might join you." Shana smirked in Leah's direction.

Leah rolled her eyes, retied her ponytail, and did a couple of high-knees. "You could have fooled me."

"Who knows? Having a couple of adrenaline junkies around all the time could land you with a few moves of your own."

"True." Leah took a few deep breaths and looked around the outdoor complex, mapping out her 'line'—a series of moves performed without breaks. "Here goes . . . "

"Nothing." Shana laughed good-naturedly and waved her on.

Leah ran to the nearest large rock, hopped onto it, then bounded to the next, tossing a smile to the girl watching her. After reaching the last rock, she leaped at the concrete wall in front of her about three feet away, her feet landing on the vertical surface first to absorb the shock of the contact, then reaching for the top of the wall to position herself into a cat leap. The soles of her new shoes scraped along the side of the wall with a satisfying crunch. She hung from the edge of the wall with her arms extended above her head, hands gripping the flat top of the wall-like structure, and her legs folded beneath her, balls of her feet glued to the side of the wall.

"Bravo on a nice cat leap."

"You know the name of the move?" Leah turned her head to stare at Shana behind her, rising from the bench.

"Of course. I could do it, too." Shana stepped to the rock Leah had just vacated and went through the same movement Leah had performed seconds earlier, landing in a similar position two feet away from Leah.

"I thought when you said you did not get it, you meant you had no idea what we were doing."

"I just don't understand how you guys could be crazy about this. Now we have to do a muscle up or jump down before our legs cramp."

"Why not do a cat-ninety?" Leah pointed a finger at the wall to the left, connected to the wall they were on at a ninety-degree angle.

"From your position, maybe. I'll have to do a muscle up."

Shana straightened one of her legs, kicked herself off the wall, and boosted herself up onto the wall in one smooth motion. "And then a turn vault."

Shana turned her body over and around the top of the wall and dropped into a cat leap on the other side.

She smirked at Leah, who was still glued on her cat leap. "Scaredy-cat? It's a slightly larger drop on this side than the barely six-foot drop on yours."

"What are you going to do?"

"Do precisions on the random slabs on this side of the wall while you mope." Shana grinned, propelling herself backward. She spun herself around in mid-air and landed cleanly on whatever it was she landed on.

Leah glanced over her shoulder, pushed away from the wall with her legs, reached out with her left foot for the wall segment, and landed in another cat leap—so-called because the traceur looks like a cat jumping toward an object while performing the move.

Somehow, Leah's foot missed the contact point and slipped from the wall. Her hand jammed into the side of the wall as she fell, throwing her off balance. There are saves and rolls in Parkour—the art of falling, called Ukemi—but it wasn't easy to roll into a Parkour safety roll *backward* while off-balance in the air.

Leah moved her right leg under her at the last minute, but managed to crash her left knee against the concrete wall as she did so, before crashing onto the ground.

Sparks—lightning-sharp jabs of pain—radiated through her knee. She reeled.

Leah looked down, doing her best to hold down a scream. Shana was having the time of her life somewhere on the other side of the wall. It would take her a while to realize that Leah was nowhere to be seen.

Her knee jerked spasmodically. She tried to stand up. The pain was not as sharp now.

Then her knee joint twisted under her weight, and she gingerly lowered herself onto the ground again.

The memories came rushing back to her. She'd never forgotten the sheer terror as her joint twisted underneath her, her knee buckling under her as she fell. The pain was bad enough, but the feeling of helplessness as the ligaments around the knee gave way had traumatized her.

Biting back the tears, Leah dragged herself toward the bench a couple of yards away.

Someone walked past, eating an apple. A red apple.

Leah looked at him, searching for a face behind the cap and sunglasses. Was that Javin?

The slight mustache was not there that last time they'd met . . . Leah's face heated as she remembered their 'discussion' and her abrupt leave.

She glanced away. She was not ready for a talk right now. All she wanted was to get her knee joint back into proper position so she could stand up. The pain of the misaligned joint was unbearable.

"Leah? Is that you? What's wrong?"

The calm, concerned voice broke through the haze of pain and shame. She opened her eyes to see Javin crouched before her, his sunglasses pushed up on his forehead, his normally reserved eyes wide with concern.

With those simple words and caring look, Leah lost her resolve and burst into tears.

"Oh dear." Javin put an arm around her shoulders, his eyes landing on the hand Leah placed on her knee.

Leah bowed her head. "I'm sorry. Please forgive me . . . my knee is hurting so bad."

"I can't hear what you're saying. You're muttering to yourself." Leah looked up and tried to smile at him.

"I'm sorry for what happened the last time . . . "

"Let's not talk about that now. Did you hurt yourself?"

Leah nodded, feeling the warmth of his arm on her back seeping into her body.

"I had a friend around—not sure where she went." Leah looked around. There was actually no sign Shana was here at all, except for the brown cooler bag and half-finished yogurt carton.

"Deserted you, eh?" Javin reached over and wiped the tears off her face. "Would you like to sit somewhere more comfortable?"

Leah nodded.

Javin left her side, stood up, and held out a hand.

"I . . . can't exactly walk right now. I think I sprained my knee."

"Oh no." He crouched behind her. "Should I carry you over to the bench?"

"Let me see if I could kick the joint back into the proper position." Leah nodded at Javin's apprehensive expression. "I've done it before." She squeezed her eyes close and forced her leg to straighten. A stab of pain traveled through her leg as the joint rolled back into place. The sharp pain subsided.

The knee would hurt and be somewhat unstable for the next week or so, but at least she should be able to walk to the car. Just to make sure, she flexed her left leg twice. Weak and painful, but still intact.

She opened her eyes. Javin was still staring at her, eyes cautious and worried.

"You okay?"

"Yes." Leah grimaced. Each sprain of her knee her left her shaken for hours, even after the pain was gone. She held out a hand to Javin. "I just need some help getting up—I should be able to walk after that."

He took her hand, brought her to a standing position, then tucked her hand into his elbow. "Lean on me if you need to, Leah." He guided her to the bench and lowered her gently onto it.

Leah's back rested against the bench, and she released a breath she didn't know she was holding. "Thanks, Javin."

"Don't mention it." He hovered over her. "Are you sure you're okay? Do we have to . . . "

Shana's voice broke in. She fast-walked toward them from the playground. "Sorry, Leah, I was gone . . . Who are you?" Shana stepped closer to Javin, eyes in slit-mode.

"A friend." Javin tilted his head to the side, eying Shana doubtfully. "And who are *you*?"

"A friend," Shana shot back.

"Some friend you are to her, leaving her on the ground alone and injured." Javin parried, both eyebrows raised.

"Now who's getting testy?" Shana hissed through clenched teeth.

"Now, now." Leah interrupted before a firefight erupted between these two. "Introduce yourselves." She waved at the two miffed nineteen-year-olds.

Shana turned on her. "Is this your secret boyfriend? Is this some sick joke about you being injured?"

Leah glanced at Javin out of the corner of her eyes. All signs of animosity he'd shown earlier were gone, and he seemed to be enjoying himself, even taking a huge bite of his apple with a mega-watt smile.

Shana, whose fisted hands rested on her hips, stood glaring down at her. Leah knew her well enough to know that the verbal beating she'd just given them was due to her frustration of not having been there to help Leah when she most needed her.

"I truly am injured." Her knee was swollen by now. "And for the record, I do not have a secret boyfriend."

"Sure doesn't look like it." Thick sarcasm there.

"Get over it, girl. Leah hurt her knee and needed someone to help her up. I just happened to be walking by and thought I would lend a hand. What's so wrong with that?" Javin rose, matching Shana's aggressive stance by crossing his arms.

Shana opened her mouth. She hesitated. Then she closed her mouth and turned away. Leah tilted her head, thoughtful. Shana never backed down from something like that before.

"We'll have to get you to the hospital. Where's your car?" Shana asked Leah, keeping her eyes away from Javin's.

"At the Vault's parking lot. I thought I would train there for a bit, then changed my mind. But . . . " Leah held up a hand when Shana shifted in that direction. "I've done this before. I know what to do. It's just a sprain. Nothing big."

"Your knee's swollen." Javin pointed to the round lump that was once her knee.

"Yeah. No more flying around for a while now." Leah grimaced.

"So you did pick up Parkour? Even after what we said?"

"Ever since then. Yes." Leah bit her lower lip. "We need to talk about what happened . . . "

"Not here, Leah." The caution was back in his voice. "We need to get you home first."

"I'll grab your car for you, Leah. We'll—I'll drive you home. This not-your-secret-boyfriend guy could go back and do whatever he was doing before he . . . "

"Shana. Stop." Leah held out her car keys. Javin snorted beside her, and Leah turned toward him. "What's so funny?"

"Never mind." He brushed a hand over his mouth. "I'm just wondering why she's so against me being your boyfriend. Did I do something wrong?"

Then he turned to Shana. "Shana. Nice name. It fits you. You're nice."

Leah's eyes danced from Shana to Javin.

Shana flashed him an annoyed glance. "That's the best you could do, Javin?" Leah was sure Shana held her head higher than usual as she sauntered away to get Leah's Jeep.

An awkward silence settled between her and Javin. A *very* awkward silence. Leah fiddled with the hem of her shorts.

Javin spoke. "Do you have something to put on your knee? Is it annoying you much?"

"I'm good. It's going to be okay."

Javin sighed, his hands gripping each other. "Look. Both of us said things we regret. Our last meeting was not the most cordial. But I was hoping we could somehow reconcile whatever rift we have between us."

Leah looked at anything but Javin's face. She studied the ground below her, the cloudless sky above, the intricate carvings of the wooden bench. "I forgive all the hurtful things you've said of me and the guy who somehow came into our conversation. I hope you'll forgive me for accusing you of being a two-sided apple. That was . . . "

"Uncalled for and false," Javin finished for her.

"Exactly." Leah looked up into a pair of understanding eyes. "Thanks for forgiving me. I was not feeling all that calm at the time."

"It was mutual." Javin smiled a little at her. Leah smiled back.

"A hug?"

"I won't mind a side hug." Leah leaned into him as he wrapped an arm around her and squeezed.

The horn of a car beeped behind them, causing them both to jump. Javin released Leah slowly, a smirk coming over his face as he watched Shana storm out of the Jeep.

"Is she always like this?" Javin turned to Leah, eyebrows raised. Quick footsteps pounded the pavement behind them.

Leah shook her head. "You guys meet for the first time, and you're both ready to fly at each other's necks. What's up with you both?"

Javin shrugged.

Shana strode up to them. "I should be asking you that question. I can't even walk down the block to get your car and drive back—less than five minutes total—without you two being all cozy together." Her eyes flashed at Leah. "I thought you had eyes only for Vic."

"That's the guy you mentioned when we were talking about . . . " Javin began, a question in his voice.

"Javin." Leah threw him a glance and turned to Shana. "I'll have you know that Javin, handsome as he is with the dark skin tone and mustache," Leah watched Shana's face closely; an eyebrow twitched, but no blushes, "is a very good friend of mine who has helped me out many times in the past. I repeat—we're good friends and nothing more."

"I'm hurt." Javin placed a hand over his heart.

Shana rolled her eyes. "Okay, okay. I understand. I'm sorry for being so up-tight. I'm just . . . flustered." She promptly turned away and pretended to fix her hair.

This time her face was definitely red, and she was obviously trying to hide it. Leah turned to Javin.

"Help me up? I'm not sure if I want to put too much weight on it for now."

He seemed lost in thought, starting at Shana. His eyes held a dreamy look, which gave way to concern as he switched his attention to her.

"Hmm? Oh, right." He called over to Shana who, having put every strand of hair in place, was making her way back to the Jeep. "Shana? Unless you want me to carry your friend romantically in public, you'd better come over and give me a hand."

Shana spun back to them. "I'm doing this only for her dignity." She stepped closer and positioned her arm around Leah's shoulders.

Javin did the same thing on Leah's other side, his arm resting over Shana's.

Leah felt a shiver on her back. Shana's? Javin's? Or both? Sparks must be flying. It would be nice if these two could . . .

" . . . Three." Shana and Javin yanked her onto her feet.

She gasped, "You guys could have warned me." Leah gingerly walked forward, grateful for the assistance.

They slowly made their way forward together. Javin shot her a look. "We did. You were miles away."

"Right." Leah gritted her teeth as she lifted her injured leg into the Jeep.

"Vic was the guy, eh? Who you said you'll never believe to be a two-sided apple?" Javin buckled Leah's seatbelt for her. Shana climbed up over the other side, and Javin promptly hopped away from Leah. Shana shook her head at him.

"Who are you calling a two-faced apple?"

"No one." Leah and Javin said in unison.

Shana pursed her lips. "I need to drive this girl home before she gives in to your overtures."

Javin lifted an eyebrow, challenging her statement.

Shana's eyes narrowed. Their stares dueled. Leah looked from one to another, amused.

A few seconds passed in silence. Shana checked her watch. "My shift starts in half an hour. And I still have to get this girl home." She glanced significantly at Javin, who nodded.

"See you around, Javin." Shana revved up the engine.

"Hopefully, we'll have a more civil conversation next time." Javin winked, then turned to Leah. "I'll bring an apple for you next time we meet."

"You owe me one—plus a visit."

"Both overdue, eh?"

"Yep."

Shana shifted gears noisily.

"Be strong." Javin looked into her eyes, holding them in his.

"Be happy." Leah smiled at the familiar farewell.

"Be you." They said together. With a smile and a wave, he turned to go.

Shana pulled out of the parallel parking spot and glanced sideways at Leah.

"You have some explaining to do, girl. Who was that, and what was all that about?"

CHAPTER SEVEN

Leah opened her eyes. The sun was shining through the east window of her apartment too brightly for it to be morning: she'd slept in.

She moved her legs. A sharp pain shot through her knee, and she relaxed back onto the futon. She was in her living room. Shana had placed an assortment of things in a semi-circle around her on the coffee table and on the floor: her phone, snacks, a bottle of water, and a stack of books. She reached over for her iPod doc, turned on some classical music, and checked her phone.

A text from Shana. "You doing okay? Do you need me to get you anything?"

"I'm fine," Leah typed back. "Thanks for yesterday."

"No problem." Shana sent her a smiley emoji.

Leah smiled to herself, laid the phone down, and took a sip of water.

Someone knocked at her door.

"Who is it?" She raised her voice, hoping whoever it was on the other side could hear her.

"Me. May I come in?"

That voice belonged only to *him*. "Vic? Is that you?"

"Yes." The lock turned, and the guy who'd been in her dreams for many a year walked in the door.

He looked just as surprised to be there as she was to see him. He held out a set of keys Leah realized were her own.

"Shana told me you were hurt. She had to rush back to work, and I took the liberty of driving your car back here for her." Leah nodded. Vic was here—truly, really, physically here. She had so many things she wanted to tell him and talk to him about: but then, what about the past was still relevant to the present? Would he remember? If he did, would he still care?

He looked at the mess around her and smiled. "Shana's doing, eh? I don't think you could make such a mess without being able to move around much."

Leah tried to loosen her tongue, but it no longer obeyed her. Perhaps it was too tired to move any more. Perhaps the cat had finally gotten her tongue. Perhaps it had something to do with the full-grown young man standing before her—just a boy when she'd last seen him. She gave Vic a vague smile and shrugged.

Vic gestured to the unoccupied half of the futon. "Do you mind?"

"Sure. Have a seat." Leah gathered the throw Shana had covered her with and cleared the empty seat.

"So . . . you've been freerunning." A feeble attempt at small talk on her part.

Vic nodded, sitting and facing her. "Thanks to you." He stretched his arms over his head and took a deep breath.

"Me? What did I do?" Leah tried to remember what she'd ever said to him on the subject: besides her brief mention of Parkour the last they've met, her mind drew a blank.

"You inspired me to look deeper into the sport. After trying it out for a few days, I couldn't let it go. And so began the last three years. On top of me working through the first three years of university."

"When I last saw you were just preparing to study, eh?"

Vic nodded. "One more year and I'll be finished. I just handed in the last exams of the past semester."

"Good for you."

"Yourself?"

"I'm working from home as a virtual bookkeeper and assistant."

"Good for you."

Small talk over, silence reigned. Leah ran her hand over the edge of her phone, while Vic fiddled his thumbs. The air weighed down with awkwardness and unspoken words.

"How's the Jung family? Is your mom doing better? Has the country air done any good to her?" Vic asked, his eyes studying her face.

"Mom has been cancer-free for two years now."

"Praise the Lord!" Genuine joy flashed in his eyes as he squeezed her hand briefly.

"Amen. I never had a chance to thank you for all you and your family did for us during those years." Leah swallowed: the pain, loneliness, dread, and uncertainty of her mother's years of battling cancer threatened to surface again. Her eyes misted over.

"Don't mention it." Vic patted her hand, then gently touched her chin and made her look at him. "We were blessed to see the active and unshakable faith your parents had in God and His will for their family." He paused, a small smile of remembrance on his face. "Shana and I wanted new friends, too. I had only Guy when my parents decided to immigrate to Canada when I was in elementary school."

"And we somehow became friends without either of us knowing much English." Leah chuckled.

Vic laughed, his eyes looking back into the past. "The talks we've had, misunderstandings, stuttering apologies and all, meant so much to my cousin and me." He turned to her again, still smiling. "How many siblings do you have again? I could only remember there was a bunch of them."

"Six. They are all doing great now." Leah smiled. "So glad we were friends with each other when we both needed a friend so badly."

"Yep." Vic nodded slowly. A few moments passed. He opened his mouth a couple of times as if about to say something, but each time he seemed to think the better of it and allowed the silence to continue between them.

"How's your family doing?" Leah shifted in her seat.

"You've met Shana and Guy. We're basically family. Mr. and Mrs. Menchaca are both doing great."

"Wonderful."

The silence that followed was broken only by their breathing and the soft music from the iPod doc nearby.

Vic turned and glanced out of the window behind him. His eyes focused on the parking lot below. "A guy is waving at you from below. Oh wait, he just left."

Leah strained to sit up. Vic gently pushed her shoulders back. "Relax. If he *is* looking for you, he'll be here soon."

"What did he look like?"

"I'm not sure. He was waving something red in his hand. An apple, maybe."

"Probably Javin. I hoped he'd drop by." Leah turned to her front door, expectant.

"Did you hope I'd drop by?" Vic's voice sounded sad, yet expectant.

Leah faced him again. She hesitated. "Yes, you, along with Guy and Shana. Maybe not Guy so much. He told me to take care of me before I went ahead and . . . "

"Leah? You in there? Is this a good time? I got your apple." A muffled voice called out behind the door.

"That's Javin. Could you let him in for me, please?" Leah smiled, hoping to take away some of the tension from his face

"Your wish is my command." Vic gave her half a grin, walked over, and opened the door.

Javin entered. "And you must be Vic." He held out a hand. Vic shook it.

"Yes. How did you guess?"

"Easy. You have Shana's eyes." Javin answered, peering around him to wave at Leah.

Leah waved back, gesturing for him to find a seat on the ground.

"You've met my cousin already?" Vic lowered himself back onto his side of the couch.

"I should say so," Javin grunted, making his way through the littered floor to get to Leah's side. "Here's your apple." He held out a perfectly ripe Honeycrisp.

"Thanks, Javin." Leah took the fruit and took a bite, her face lighting up with pleasure. "I appreciate it."

Vic gave her a what's-this-all-about look but kept his mouth shut. Javin cleared a spot beside her on the floor and sat, his head touching the armrest Leah's shoulder rested on.

"How did you get in? Do you live here?" Vic asked, looking wary.

"The age-old trick. Slipping in close behind a patron." Javin tossed Vic a smirk. "Yourself?"

"Same." Vic laughed, winked at him, then sobered. "So how did you know my . . . "

"Leah! Open up! We're here!"

"Shana," Leah noted, nodding to Vic.

In an instant, Javin was on his feet, a smile stretched across his face. "I'll get it." He pulled the door open.

"It's you again." Shana's biting tone was the polar opposite of the positive greeting she'd called out seconds ago. "I should have expected you to hang around anyways."

"It's great to see you again, Shana," Javin replied in a cheery tone. "You're looking great, as usual."

Shana shot him a death glare and strode past him.

"And who is this gentleman?" Javin held out a hand to the lean-figured guy Shana had brought.

"My name is Guy."

"So is mine, on occasion," Javin laughed, his eyes darting to the two hands Guy kept in his jeans pocket.

Guy's brows drew together. "No, I mean it. It's my first name."

"Nice to meet you, Guy." Javin shrugged.

"I wish I could say the same, but we'll have to find out." Guy finally reached out his long fingers and shook Javin's hand.

Leah frowned to herself. "Shana? Did you and Guy had an argument of sorts?"

"No. Why?" Shana shot her a glance, her strident tone leaving her voice. But before Leah could swallow the bite of apple she had in her mouth just then, Shana's eyes narrowed. "Is that from him?" Shana demanded, jerking a thumb in Javin's direction. Leah glanced over at the two uncomfortable-looking guys standing side-by-side a couple of paces away. Javin raised an eyebrow at Shana's motions. Leah shook her head at him.

"Yes, Shana. What's wrong with that?"

Shana looked about the room. "I thought you were just 'friends.' Then every time I turn around, you guys have something else going on."

Vic opened his mouth to interpose. "Shana. Calm down. This is not like you to blow up . . . "

"Shana. It's only an inside joke Leah has with me."

Shana turned on Javin, who'd stepped forward to try to explain. "Some kind of inside joke, huh? As if you guys could have . . . "

Guy spoke. "Shana. That's enough."

Leah thanked Guy with a glance. She cleared her throat. "Maybe we all should properly introduce ourselves. Having all four of you visit at the same time was totally unexpected, but we'll do our best to work around that without any hurt feelings."

"If that's the case, I better leave now." Shana rose from where she about to sit. Leah thought for a moment, trying to see things from Shana's eyes. That was it. Every available spot was close to Javin.

"Shana. You could sit between Guy and Vic over to the left."

"I'll be where that *Javelin's* target would be."

"All the better for that *Javelin* to . . . "

"Could you just stop?" Shana turned away from him.

Javin shrugged it off, but Leah could tell Shana's sharp tone hurt him deeper than he'd want to admit.

Vic and Guy looked at Leah expectantly, as if daring her to clear this mess.

"Let's just give each other a brief bio of our lives."

"And our resumes and photo ID?" Vic joked. Leah and Javin chuckled. The tension in the air loosened.

Javin raised his hand. "Whatever you have, bro. I'll go ahead."

"And that about wraps me up." Guy looked at Leah, his eyes unreadable. Leah nodded.

Javin looked at his watch. "I guess I'd better get going. I've got a job interview—two, actually."

"Doing what?" Shana stretched herself, her eyes on Javin.

"Softball coaching for elementary school kids. The other one is probably some office work. Computer-related."

"Hmm." Shana got up, nodding.

"I guess this is where we take our leave." Guy stood up. Leah looked around at each of them.

"Let me see you all to the door." Leah pushed herself up to her feet, then winced as her sore knee took some of her body weight. Vic was at her side in an instant. He gave her a gentle smile and offered his arm.

"Let me help you."

"Thanks." She slipped her hand into the crook of his elbow and leaned on him as they headed toward the small foyer. "I'm glad all of you got to know each other a little." She smiled at her friends, all looking at her with varying degrees of concern.

"It was not too hard to get comfortable—a little more comfortable—with each other, since we have a few important things in common," Javin added, moving to the door. "Having you as a friend, having a passion for Parkour, and having Christ as Savior and Lord." He counted off three fingers, looking at each person with a smile.

"We should train with each other sometime," Guy spoke after a moment of silence.

Out of the corner of her eye, she saw Vic glare at Guy. Guy shrugged back at him, an uncomfortable expression on his face. Vic turned to her. "We'll wait for you to get better first, Leah. No worries."

Leah smiled, losing herself in the concern expressed in those brown eyes. "I could tag along and watch you guys. We could have fun together, despite this." She pointed at her injured knee.

"I'm open anytime next weekend, if any of you are?" Javin looked around. Four nods greeted his question.

"Next Saturday it is. I can't wait to train—watch you guys train—together." Leah smiled.

CHAPTER EIGHT

THAT SUNDAY . . .

Leah moved her laptop toward her and pulled up one of her favorite recorded sermons. Clicking the file open, she joined into the prayer as the pastor prayed for the congregation and for all tuning in.

The message was uplifting, convicting, and inspiring. Brother David touched on what each of us could do to be light and salt in a community—by living out redeemed lives that are being constantly sanctified by the Holy Ghost.

The reverend's closing statements snagged her attention. Looking straight at the camera—straight at her—Brother David asked this question: "If there is something God has given you—a gift, a dream, a vision—that you could use to spur others on for God's glory and his kingdom, you better start moving if you haven't already. Is there something in your community that you could do to make a difference—in the lives of young people, or old, or the tiny? Something that you have been placed where you are, with the people you know around you, that could be used for God?"

The prayer they'd uttered afterward was lost to Leah. In the vortex of thoughts and ideas that suddenly filled her mind there was one central idea, the beginnings of a life-long vision.

Pastor Michael's voice came to mind. She'd talked with the pastor a couple of times after that Daniel meeting. "Leah, God could use anything you have to offer Him, and turn it into a blessing for others. That means anything you do, say, or make. But the point is, you have to do something about it. You have to work. You have to sacrifice. You have to give. But if you are truly doing what God plans for you with the talents He's bestowed on you; He'll bless you in unbelievable ways."

Leah clung to those words as an idea grew in her mind—the accumulation of the time spent thinking and praying the three days she had been homebound.

God could use anything and anyone for His glory, for the expansion of His kingdom. What if Parkour could touch the lives of teens in her area? Overcoming obstacles was the essence of the sport. What if this, along with the discipline, hard work, and perseverance the sport demands, could trigger positive outcomes in the lives of teens? Knowing that obstacles could be overcome was the first step. Fears had to be overcome. There had to be confidence. Training. Faith.

What if Parkour could help someone like Paul get back on their feet after their dreams have been destroyed? Though his progress might be slower, the act of overcoming physical obstacles might guide him toward overcoming his inner obstacles—mental, emotional, psychological, and so on.

She set her cup on the coffee table and turned off the sermon video.

Tingles ran down her spine at the thought. Perhaps she could start a team of young people, passionate about Jesus, this sport, and helping others toward the light. They could work together to change the lives of others through Parkour and the Gospel. Help them achieve their God-given potential instead of living in sin and fear.

A vision—it sounded impossible, but she could not shake the idea off.

They would call themselves Team Set Free.

CHAPTER NINE

THAT SATURDAY . . .

"Would you like to sit on that bench?" Vic pointed, a gentle hand on her shoulder as he guided her toward the seat. Leah blinked against the bright sunlight to look into his face and nodded. She took a step, a pebble rolled under her heel, and she stumbled.

"Careful." Vic gripped her shoulders and gently steered her to the bench.

"Thanks." Leah sat and reached for the purse on Vic's shoulder. He handed it to her, smiling.

"My pleasure. Is there anything I can get you before the show starts?"

"A camera, maybe?" Leah teased. Vic laughed, throwing his head back.

Shana, Guy, and Javin walked toward them from different directions. Leah glanced at the threesome, wondering why they were so quiet after having carpooled over. At least Shana and Javin were not at each other's throats—for now.

"Hey guys." Leah waved.

"Hey boss." Javin tossed her a smirk and looked at Vic, who stood beside Leah as if to protect her. "Vic."

"Javin. It's nice to see my competitor in such buff condition." The dry sarcasm enlisted a chuckle from Leah. Javin was indeed the most well-muscled of the three young men, with Vic being of average build and Guy tall and lean.

"Who said anything about competitions?" Leah grinned at Shana.

"The guys did. When we were leaving your apartment last week." Shana deposited her purse beside Leah's, giving each of the assembled guys a once-over. Out of the corner of her eye, Leah saw Javin stretch taller and flex his biceps when Shana's gaze landed on him. Leah turned to Vic, smiling.

He immediately struck an alpha dog pose.

Guy just stood there, taking in the testosterone play at hand. He turned to Leah. "Didn't I tell you to be careful?"

"Yeah. I did my best." Guy raised his eyebrows at her. "Do you think I want to miss training for three weeks?" Leah turned her head to the sun, closing her eyes and taking a deep breath. "Trust me; it's hard enough to keep the smile on."

Guy held up a hand, eyes probing, head tilted. "Did you take painkillers?"

"Don't need them, why take them?" Leah shrugged a shoulder.

"That's the spirit, girl." Guy paused. "I'm sorry you got injured, but are you this stubborn every time someone tells you to not do something for your own good?" Guy threw her a lop-sided grin.

"Yes, I am." Leah shot back with a smile. "You better hurry up. The two other guys are raring to go."

She gestured to Javin and Victor a few yards away, warming up with stretches while chewing each other out verbally. Shana swigged a water bottle and smacked Vic on the arm with it after he said something that clearly did not settle well with her. Javin laughed, the sound floating back to Leah on a gentle breeze.

Guy knelt on the ground to tie his shoes. "I have nothing to worry about. No girl for me to impress over here." Guy stood and touched his toes in a hamstring stretch.

"No girls for you to impress . . . you're implying those two over there do. Interesting thought."

"You haven't noticed Shana's changed? Javin over there touched a chord in her that left her all jumpy and dreamy. Even the patrons at Panera Bread have noticed her wider smile and jitteriness."

"I thought her on-my-toes thing was only when they met." Leah moved her left knee to keep it from freezing in place.

"Apparently not. Her boss had to remind her to be careful when handing out bowls of soup and what not."

Leah looked at the group over by the kids' playground. Vic and Javin were pointing at different structures and arguing—probably about the route each of them was going to take. Something Guy said earlier bothered her.

"You say Javin is trying to impress Shana. You have no one. And Vic has . . . "

Guy shrugged again, his eyes landing on her for one searching glance before he sauntered away to join the group. "He never got over you."

Shana outlined the route the guys were to take.

"See that wall over there? Climb over that, do precisions on the rocks till you reach those monkey bars." She pointed to the older-kids playground on her left. "Do a bar lache. Get yourself on top of those bars, walk on top to the rails around the slide there, precision from one rail to the next—or you can fast-walk on the rails if you have super balance—and backflip—no, make that double backflip—off the end of that walkway."

"You guys would sprint all the way from where you land over to that splash park . . . "

"I did not sign up to get wet, Shana!" Javin whined.

"Then move so fast even water can't touch you." Shana shot back without as much as a glance at him. "All will crawl under those toddler-sized structures—no knees touching the ground, use your quadrupedal movement skills to get through that—then touch that arbor behind the water buckets thingy in the splash park. Fastest one wins.

"On the way back, you guys will compete in a creativity contest, which will be judged by myself and Leah. All the way from that arbor back to this spot. Use everything you've got. Surprise us."

Shana paused, glancing at Leah. Leah nodded. This was going to be great!

"Guys, on the count of three."

Javin crouched into a pre-leap position, Guy stepped one leg back and bent his front knee in a sprinting-prep position. Vic held up a hand, braced himself, and threw a backflip.

Guy glanced over at Leah and rolled his eyes good-naturedly.

"One, two, three!!" Shana shouted and dropped her raised arm.

Like three shots from a firing squad, the guys dove at the wall, performed perfect wall-runs and climb-ups, and turn-vaulted over to the other side of the wall.

Shana followed them at a leisurely pace. Leah got up from her seat, took a few hesitant steps, and made her way to the side of the wall to watch the three friends hopping their way to the kid's playground. At some point, Vic looked up and around and caught her eye. A smile grazed his face, and he put extra effort into performing a perfect precision jump onto the next concrete slab. Jump complete, he paused to look back at Leah. She smiled. "You're losing time! Keep going!"

Her encouraging yell attracted the attention of several other couples who'd chosen this time of the day—high noon—to walk hand-in-hand around the park. A woman and another couple lingered to watch the three young men hop, run, and jump like hyped-up monkeys around and on the kid's playground.

"Do those guys know that that's for kids?" The sardonic tone grated on Leah's nerves. She turned to the well-dressed couple who'd paused in their afternoon walk to watch them. Leah made an effort to keep a smile on her face.

"They're aware of that, ma'am. They just choose to use it in unusual ways. Look." Leah lifted a hand to point at Javin, who was about to perform a double backflip from the edge of the walkway of the playground.

"That guy's nuts." The other woman shook her manicured finger at Javin. Leah chose not to comment on that and made sure Javin landed safely before she turned to address the fashionably-dressed woman.

"Watch what the other guys do."

Vic was right behind Javin. He braced himself on the rail and leaped into the air, slanting backward and using the momentum in his knees to rotate him once, twice in the air. Leah shouted and clapped her hands, hoping he could hear her from here.

Guy was next. He calmly stepped onto the rail, swung his arms languidly, and then effortlessly threw himself back into a triple back-flip, landing clean on the balls of his two feet. In a split second, he was sprinting after Vic and Javin.

Leah was impressed. She could perform a double only on a good day. Guy made three rotations look easy. She let out a whistle.

The couple muttered something about insane risk-takers and moved to the side.

Leah understood where they were coming from. She'd felt the same way at first. Why would people be willing to risk their limbs or lives for the thrill of movement? Her mother and sisters had more or less accepted her passion for Parkour, but still they were skeptical. Should she be doing this so much, so often?

"We want to know what our bodies are capable of for ourselves. Tough training tends to increase confidence." Leah would fire back at skeptics. "That's why we push and train ourselves so much." They would shake their head and leave her alone.

A shout near the arbor yanked Leah from her musings. Apparently, Guy had not only caught up to the two competing guys, but also passed them to win the speed-race. Leah clapped and hooted.

The group shared back-slaps and laughter as they made their way back to her.

"These boys would have lunch before the creativity competition," Shana explained as the group sat in a semi-circle on the ground around Leah. Shana gestured at Guy and Javin, pulling out sandwiches and wraps from their respective backpack and duffel bag.

"It's awkward sitting above you guys," Leah mumbled, shifting in her seat.

"I'll sit beside you. Then we could feel awkward together." Vic moved to the empty seat beside her and took out a hamburger and a take-out container of poutine. The aroma of French fries, melted cheese, and brown gravy tickled Leah's nose.

"Smells delicious."

Vic nodded, digging a fork into his food. "You brought your lunch?"

Leah looked around her. "Um. I don't think so. It's not that easy to cook when you have to sit down every few minutes or so." She brushed away Vic's concerned look with a smile. "I'm fine. I should have an energy bar in my purse. If not . . . Javin, would you happen to have an extra apple somewhere?"

"As a matter of fact, I do." He dug in his backpack for a while and came up with a Granny Smith. "It's not the right color, but I hope it's good enough."

Leah accepted it with a small smile. "It will do. Thanks."

"You're welcome, boss."

"Boss? Where did that come from?"

"This apple thing, too." Guy pointed out helpfully.

Leah exchanged awkward glances with Javin. Shana poked Vic's leg, her eyes on Javin, who sat facing her on the ground.

Shana coughed. "Much as we'd like to hear you two out, I'm starving, and we better pray soon before something bad happens."

"Go ahead, Shana." Javin looked relieved.

"Who's the oldest here? That's you, right, Vic?"

"All of twenty-one and three quarters now." Vic pantomimed patting himself on the back. "Shana's nineteen, Guy's twenty, and Leah's twenty, so that leaves you, sir." He nodded at Javin. "You're the only guy here with a beard."

"It's not a beard, it's a mustache." Javin touched the sparse facial hair above his upper lip. "I'm nineteen. You're in the hot seat here, Vic. Go ahead."

"Let us pray." The group bowed their heads as Vic offered a simple thanks for the wonderful day, for friends, and prayed a blessing over the food.

They dug in. Leah bit into the apple, the tangy flavor of Granny Smith apples pervading her mouth. She nodded at Javin. "Answer their questions, bro. That's an order."

Javin dipped his head. "As you wish, boss." He cleared his throat, swallowed his bite of chicken wrap, and then looked up at Leah, his eyes smiling. "Do you want me to tell them how you were my boss for three weeks *and* stole my apple after I'd served you so well?"

"That won't be necessary, Javin," Leah coughed and motioned to the rest of the group. "Sorry, inside joke. We met at a summer camp a few years ago."

Guy nodded carefully, then trained his eyes on Leah's, silently probing. He finished his sandwich without taking his eyes off hers.

"You got something on your mind."

Leah stared at him. "Do I look strange or something?"

"Nothing's wrong with you. You just look like you have something going on in your head that you can't wait to share." Guy shrugged, his eyes glued onto her face.

"She'd be smiling and laughing if that was the case." Shana narrowed her eyes at Leah.

"She's nervous." Vic's voice was soft.

"Guys! Stop talking about me as if I'm not here." Leah wrapped the apple core in a tissue and tossed it to Guy, who caught it and stuck it inside his used sandwich wrapper. "Fine. I do have an idea I want to share to see what you all think. And yes, I'm nervous because I haven't thought everything out yet, and I'm not sure if it works."

"All ears." Javin crossed his legs.

"Here. This tastes really good." Vic held out the dish of poutine. It *looked* good, *smelled* good, but could not possibly *be good*. "To calm your nerves before you begin your speech."

"Who said anything about a speech?" Leah joked back, shaking her head at the proffered food.

"I know it's not organic and healthy, but it sure beats that tiny apple you had. Here."

Vic lifted a bite of poutine and held it out toward her. She hesitated. An awkward beat passed. Guy cleared his throat.

"Thanks but no thanks, Vic. You know me." Leah smiled at his insistent teasing.

One side of his mouth lifted. "It's *so* good." He took a bite and groaned. "Your loss is my gain."

"Whatever."

"Your idea, Leah?" Guy prompted, squatting on his heels. "It includes us as a team, eh?"

"You just read my mind. How did you do that?" Leah raised an eyebrow. "It does. Do you think the five of us could change the lives of teens using Parkour?"

Shana tilted her head but stayed silent. Javin asked, "How? You mean teaching them how to do Parkour?"

Leah nodded. Vic ran his index finger and thumb down the sides of his face as if stroking his non-existent beard. "How would that change lives? It's just a sport."

Leah paused. They needed to know how she reached this idea. "Three weeks ago, I was driving home from work. Suddenly, this young man ran out and threw himself onto the road in front of my Jeep."

Shana gasped, covering her mouth with her hand.

"I slammed on the brakes just in time. I got out, helped him up, and walked with him back to the sidewalk, where his distraught mother told me what happened." Leah took a sip of water from Guy's proffered water bottle. "The gist of the story was, Paul had just visited the doctor, who told him that he was never going to compete in triathlons again due to complications from an injury last year."

"That must be tough to swallow," Vic noted. Leah nodded.

"He could not see a way out of his broken dreams, so he chose death. Thank God I was able to stop the car in time."

"Amen." Javin took Shana's sandwich wrapper and stuffed it into his own fist.

"How does this relate to your idea?" asked Guy.

"Good question. The way I see it is this. This boy is facing multiple obstacles in his life, just like many others. They're trapped. They're stuck behind their fears, their past, their hurts. Parkour, as we all know, teaches that all obstacles can be overcome, with dedication, perseverance, and discipline. This sport itself cannot change the whole person, or set the person completely free: only Jesus can do that. But this could be a step in the right direction for people who need to be set free."

"But why this? It's a nice idea and sounds very exciting, but could Parkour really change lives the way you're telling us it could?" Shana propped her chin on her knees, eyes on Leah.

"Did it change yours?" Leah challenged. Shana shrugged.

"It changed mine. Before I began to practice Parkour seriously, I was a self-conscious, stressed-out mess. I worried about how I looked, what people thought of me. And there were fears: what I could do and could not do. What I wanted to do but held back from because of fear, because it seemed too impossible, because I was not good enough to meet whatever standards I was held to. Know what I mean?"

"You're saying Parkour helped you overcome those fears and self-restrictions?" Guy asked.

"In some ways, yes. Having decided to make this sport a big part of my life, I had to accept that I would not be perfect. I can never please everyone. Instead of trying to live up to other people's standards and ideas of what my life should look like and be like, I'll live out God's plan for me and do what he'd created me to do." Leah paused to organize her thoughts. "One important thing Parkour has shown me is that, with dedication, persistence, and hard work, mental and physical obstacles *can* be overcome. That is what kicked off the idea in my head. People need to know they are capable of overcoming obstacles in life."

"Especially teens nowadays." Javin's voice was thoughtful.

"How would this work out, though? As a non-profit outreach ministry, or more like a business? What's the target age-range? How would we work this out around our own schedules and the schedules of the people we're trying to help? Where do we teach or train? What do we *do*, really?" Guy's questions erupted at her like machine-gun fire.

"Hey, hey, hey." Leah held up a hand. "I haven't worked through the details myself yet. It's just an idea. But I think that, with our mismatching work schedules, and with all of us being single—"

"At least for now," Vic interposed seriously.

"What do you mean by that?" Leah gave him a strange look.

"I just mean that you never know. But never mind." He waved for her to continue.

Leah shrugged it off. "I'm thinking only weekday evenings and weekends work, basically. And while I was thinking more of a non-profit teen outreach type of thing, Guy, your point about the possibility of turning this into a business of sorts is possible, though I don't see how we'll be able to compete with the Parkour classes offered by the Vault down the street."

"If you're planning to do all this outdoors, you're definitely at a business disadvantage. Moms tend to want their kids to stay in one piece, and matted gyms sound better than the unforgiving concrete and dirt we have here. I'm assuming that you'll want to get the kids here and teach them?" Javin gestured at the park they were in.

"It's the best alternative I could see. And yes, I'm taking Parkour back to the outdoor urban environment from which it was stolen by the indoor facilities. We could use the Vault for bad weather days if necessary."

"The occasional cuts and scrapes would teach the teens about personal responsibility, hard work, and patience when it comes to persistent training in progressions and moves." Guy sent Leah a pointed look.

"Exactly. You're starting to catch onto the idea."

"Just trying to see this from your point of view." Guy waved away the compliment. "It sounds like a great idea, but I'll have to give it some thought." Guy got up and headed over to a nearby recycle bin, garbage in hand.

"Would it work, though? Would people actually want to come, send their kids here for a couple of hours each week to learn what many consider a dangerous sport?" Shana spoke up. "There are the parents to consider. Also, what worked for you might not be what would help the other kids."

Javin nodded.

Leah was silent. They were right. She'd thought about it, prayed about it, spoken about it on the spur of the moment, the only evidence she could give for her argument being her own transformation. But was that not strong enough?

"Did training build and shape you as a person, Javin and Shana?" Leah measured her words.

Javin shifted his position and stared at a spot on the ground. "It helped take my mind off the death of my brother and grandfather when they passed away in a head-on collision one year ago. I was able to channel my anger and sorrow into movement instead of yelling at my parents, my one living brother, or the drunk driver whom we later visited in the local jail." He paused. "It made a difference in my life. Besides being the one thing I found shelter and comfort in other than God during that dark time, it kept me fit and made me feel alive."

Shana reached over and touched Javin's arm. "I'm so sorry, Javin."

Leah nodded in sympathy. "I had no idea you were going through that when we had our argument, Javin. I apologize."

Javin nodded, patting Shana's hand. "It's okay. Time heals wounds, albeit slowly and never completely." He took a moment before nodding to Shana. "Your turn."

Shana took her hand away from Javin's arm and spoke in a subdued tone. "I don't have anything that touching or deep to share. I basically went along with this big guy here," she stuck a thumb at Vic, "on whatever crazy moves or tricks he was doing with his buddy, Guy. From following them around and accepting their dares, I grew to love the sport and trained every chance I got."

Guy returned, and noting the sober faces, sat down without a word, shooting a confused glance at Vic.

"We're sharing about how Parkour touched or changed our lives." Vic clarified. "I think you can say I started doing this because I wanted to impress Le . . . this girl who introduced this sport to me a couple of years back. And from the first day of training, I was hooked, and never looked back."

Leah nodded, her throat suddenly tight.

They all looked at Guy. "Me? I could not let that guy over there leave me in his dust. We've been busy sharpening each other ever since."

They laughed.

"Maybe give us all a day or two to think and pray about this?" Shana suggested, rising from the ground in one fluid motion. Javin and Guy both got up. Vic remained seated beside Leah.

"It's a good idea with lots of potential. A combination of Parkour training and evangelism—am I right?" Vic lowered his head to look directly into her eyes.

"Yup."

"But would it work the way we're hoping it would? Could Parkour actually change the lives of the people?"

They were living proof. She was living proof. But could they help others towards living a set-free life, free from sin by the grace and power of God, free from fears through confidence and persistence, free from the inability to overcome obstacles through hard work and training? She knew it would work. But she could not prove it. Yet.

"There's only one way to find out." Leah looked around the group. They nodded.

CHAPTER TEN

"Don't you need to be working or studying, maybe take a summer term?" Leah spoke into her phone in reply to Vic's offer to drive her to the physiotherapist's clinic.

"The last school term just ended last week, so I basically have the entire summer off for work or to take care of you, since you don't seem to be doing too good a job doing that." Vic made a *tsk tsk* sound.

"I don't need to be babysat. I can hobble around fine." She hesitated. Silence from his end. She pushed on. "It's been a while now. I've done this before."

Vic took a deep breath. "Leah, I'm heading over to your place in a few minutes. Look for Shana's blue sedan. And I promise to be a perfect gentleman."

Why could he put his finger on exactly why she hesitated about letting him drive her to the clinic fifteen minutes away? She sighed into the phone, wondering why he was so persistent.

"Maybe I could call Shana or . . ."

"Shana's busy serving overfed patrons at Panera Bread; I just dropped her off. It's her afternoon shift. Guy is working a gig at the software company across the street from where I am. That will take him all day. And before you ask, Javin got a call from an old school friend and just texted me to make sure you go where you have to safely: he would not be able to make it."

"I'm glad you all clicked." Leah bit into a freshly peeled banana in her hand.

More silence.

"You better be ready. I'm headed to your place right now. You're already late. I know how crazy the traffic could be."

"So do I." She paused, deliberating. "Fine, you win. I'll come with you. But just this once."

"I've taken care of you before. You and your family." Vic's voice was quiet. She heard him inhale deeply. "I could take care of you again."

Leah held her breath, laid down her banana, then leaned her elbows down on the countertop and gently exhaled. "We could leave the past alone, Vic. I'm more than grateful for what you've done for us. But we're not teens anymore. We can't . . . you wouldn't . . . "

Vic sighed. "Leah, let's not talk about that for now." He sounded sad, defeated.

Leah frowned to herself. "I'll be waiting for you in the foyer on ground level."

"See you in a few." The call ended. Vic's words nagged at her, but she forced her mind to move on and shrugged away her confusion. Leah took careful steps to dispose of her banana peel. She filled a water bottle and went to the bathroom to freshen up, then caught herself trying to create a fancy hairdo. For goodness sake, she was just going to the physiotherapist's! No need to fancy up.

Giving her hair a simple ponytail and straightening her blouse and khaki capris, Leah grabbed her purse from the chair in the foyer and opened the door, locking it behind her.

The trip down the elevator was uneventful and lonely. But the moment the elevator doors opened to reveal Vic standing before her, waiting in all his casual jeans and t-shirt glory, all the boring thoughts fled. She stepped forward with a smile and allowed Vic to escort her to the sedan waiting outside.

"Be careful." Vic held her elbow as she stumbled to the bed the receptionist pointed out to them. Leah stepped up to the black mattress and turned her back to it, pulling herself onto the bed.

She reached to take her sneakers off. Vic immediately knelt down and gently slipped her shoes off for her. Leah blushed, feeling being too well-taken care of. He looked up and smiled at her, holding her eyes with a warm, calm gaze. "Leah, I want to tell you that . . . "

"Not now. Not here, Vic," she whispered, pleading. She did know what he was going to say. But if their conversation on the phone was any indication, she wasn't ready to deal with the confusing thoughts and hopes that have somehow revived in her heart. Not yet.

He looked confused. Then he gently pushed her hand away. "I was just about to tell you that I enjoyed our chat in the car coming over here. It was great to see where God has been taking both of us the few years we've been apart."

Leah exhaled and smiled. "I enjoyed it, too. It's amazing how the years have passed, and so much has changed. We've both grown up some."

Vic tucked her socks back into place, smiled up at her, and nodded. "But some things haven't changed, I hope." He stood and held her eyes in his for a few seconds. Then he looked at her legs with concern, apparently willing to let the subject drop for the time being.

"Are you able to swing your leg up?"

"I think so." Leah scooted backward and pulled her left leg up after her right. "Thank you so much for bringing me, Vic."

"You're welcome." He gave her a smile, waved, and left. She noticed that his steps lacked their usual spring. Even his smiles seemed sad. What was wrong with him? This wasn't the Vic she remembered. He'd been enigmatic and quietly sorrowful when they'd met in her apartment after being years apart. He was no longer the cheerful, optimistic, carefree young man she'd known. Was it simply because they've both grown up? Was it her fault?

Leah sighed.

A tiny Korean-looking woman walked up beside her bed and reached over to pull the curtains closed, forming a curtained-off room with only herself and Leah.

"How are we today?" The accented voice spoke cheerily to Leah. Small, leathery hands gently nudged the hem of her capris upwards.

"I'm doing well."

"Good, good. That was your boyfriend? Husband?"

"Just a friend."

"I see." The little woman focused on her knee for a while. She moved the patella left to right, up and down. "There's still some swelling. Have you been doing your exercises?"

"Yes, three to four times a day."

"Good. Let's check our range of motion; then we'll do some pushing and pulling to give your knee more mobility."

"Sounds great!" The procedure was familiar. Leah hoped that this time her knee would hurt less than her previous and more serious injury years ago. *Don't go there. Stay in the present.*

The physiotherapist squirted a generous amount of rubbing cream into her hand, then begin to massage Leah's knee. "Let's try to get the swelling down before we move on to other things."

Leah nodded, focusing on the soothing motions of the cool hands on her knee. The relaxing activity was over too soon.

"I'm going to ask you to bend your knee as much as you can so I can measure the angle of the bend."

Leah complied. After a few minutes, the woman checked her notes. "You gained fifteen degrees. I told you this sprain would heal quickly."

"I've been doing the exercises as you have commanded, oh mighty therapist."

The woman giggled. "You're funny." She motioned to another therapist. "This girl here can work with her machines now."

"The TENS or ultrasound?" the blonde-haired girl asked.

"TENS will be enough. For fifteen minutes."

The younger therapist nodded, gave Leah a smile, and silently connected the Transcutaneous Electrical Nerve Stimulator to a power source, carefully attached two pair of rubber pads to the sides of Leah's knee with the help of some tape, then turned the machine on. "That's good?"

"Yes, thanks so much, Brie."

The girl nodded, "You're welcome," and headed over to another bed to care for another patient.

Trying to ignore the zaps of electricity stimulating her knee joint, Leah leaned back on the raised bed and took out her phone, hoping to pass the time somewhat productively.

An email from Pastor Michael stood out from the others in her inbox.

She clicked on the email and read through his answer to the question she had about the passage their Bible study group had worked with the Sunday she'd missed. He'd been kind enough to send her a copy of his lesson notes, and she'd been thinking through it.

Her eyes dropped to the bottom of the email. With raised eyebrows, she read,

> Javin told me you were thinking of starting up something in your area. I asked Javin for details. Leah, I'd thought you were ambitious, but this blew through all the limits I thought you had. It might just be the thing teens—especially teens that have been hurt before in some way—need today. Javin shared briefly about how each of your team members had been improved and impacted by this tremendous sport. I'll be praying for you as you seek His direction for you and this vision.
> In His service,
>
> Pastor Michael

Leah bowed her head and prayed. She felt a calmness and peace sweep over her as the vision solidified in her mind and anchored itself in her heart.

Team Set Free had better get moving. They must start training and practicing even harder themselves, and mock-training each other to get themselves primed for teaching others.

She could not wait.

CHAPTER ELEVEN

NEXT SATURDAY . . .

"All set?"

Vic and Javin looked at Leah, who sat on the wall she'd fallen off of four weeks ago. The physio told her to go easy on the leg—though she did not have to go back for checkups, she could not join in her team's mock-teaching.

"Yeah, boss." Javin drawled, looking at Guy and Shana, who'd chosen to pose like spoiled teenagers as Leah explained her plan for training each other as practice. Three things were absolute prerequisites for any Parkour teacher—patience, experience, and good communication. These they would practice and train.

"All right, Jav. Teach Shana how to do the three basic vaults over that low wall." Leah pointed to a four-foot-tall brick wall jutting out from the side of the one she was sitting on. "That would be the lazy, speed, and turn vault. After that, you can guide her through the Kong vault—but take it easy on that one. Make sure she doesn't smash her knee caps."

"Got it, boss."

"I know I'm acting like one, but I'm not your boss, Javin. Cut it out." Leah pursed her lips and tilted her head at him, eyes unblinking.

Javin shrugged, smirking. "Whatever you say, boss-Leah."

Leah rolled her eyes and turned to Vic. "Vic, take Guy over to those logs and teach him precisions and bounding. After that, get him to do handstands and handsprings—against the wall if needed."

"As you wish, m'lady." Vic bowed from the waist.

"What's wrong with you guys?" Leah grumbled, shifting to a more comfortable position. Sharp pebbles ground themselves under her, but she ignored the pain and focused on the two interesting scenes unfolding before her.

Javin was energetically throwing his arms and legs over the brick structure, verbally explaining each movement and demonstrating them to Shana, who crossed her arms. She was playing the bored, spoiled teen to the tilt. Javin finally performed a normal lazy vault over the low wall at normal speed, then motioned for Shana to copy him. Shana stood beside the wall, swung one leg up, effortlessly sat on top of the wall, swung both legs up, and dropped to a stand on the ground on the other side.

"Shana . . . that's not realistic enough," Leah called down. "Try to do it as if this was your very first time. Give it another try."

Shana sighed and pretended to be unable to swing her leg high enough to get her body over the wall—which gave Javin an excuse to grab Shana's foot and show her how it should be done.

Shana swatted Javin's hands away and gave her leg a few more swings before finally getting one leg high enough to clear the wall.

Then comes the momentum. Then the control of the moment. Then the coordination of hand and arm support as the body passed over the wall mid-air. And from the speed of learning Shana had chosen to exhibit, that would take another good while.

She shifted her attention to the two "best buddies." Vic had placed two twigs two feet apart and was demonstrating a proper precision-jump form to know-it-all Guy. Vic swung his arms and jumped from one stick, landing on the balls of his feet on the other.

He motioned for Guy to take a try. Guy bent his knees low, pushed off, and landed with his legs too far apart, breaking the uneven twig in two.

Vic and Guy laughed together. Vic was a natural at things like this, Leah mused as her mind's imagination took her years away into the future, in this same place.

She could see happy people—adults, teens, and kids alike—finding freedom and joy in motion on these very grounds. Fresh air, friendships, and freerunning. What a great combination.

"Leah? Do you want a hand down?" Javin looked up at her, holding out a hand.

"That would not be enough, Javin. I think I need two hands." Leah shot him a wry smile.

"The best hands to help you are at the ends of your two arms." Guy loosely quoted, his tone dry.

"I need four then." Leah countered good-humoredly.

"Here." Vic stepped up and held out his arms. "Jump. I'll catch you."

"Should I risk it? What if . . . I hit the ground with my bad leg before . . . ?"

"Trust him, Leah. And stop thinking of yourself as weak and injured. You're stronger than you think. If you think you're weak, you'll be weak for the rest of your life." Shana looked down at her from her position, standing on the wall Leah was seated on.

"You're a wise girl, Shana." She gave her friend a smile and turned to Vic.

"Here I come!"

Vic widened his stance and grinned up at her. The dimples reminded her of those lonely, uncertain years, back in the days when a friendly smile from a certain boy always took her breath away. Leah hesitated, unwilling to revive those memories. He'd never know, and she'll let things stay that way.

"Do I have to push you down?" Shana matched action to her words, and Leah found herself letting out a yelp of surprise as her body left the wall and fell toward the ground.

Just before her feet touched the hard concrete, strong arms held her close. "I've got you. Relax." The softly-accented voice by her ear made that impossible. She found her footing and pulled back. Vic's arms left her side. "You okay?"

She nodded, looking at the three other people gathered around her.

"Would you guys please stop fussing over me?"

"I did not bother to. It's all your own fault." Guy walked away, his backward glance betraying his concern.

"Just don't want you to hurt yourself. That's all. Shana?" Javin motioned to the girl still on the wall. "Did you bring some snacks?"

"For you hungry monkeys?" The shadow at Leah's feet nodded. "Race you to my car."

The two sprinted away, and suddenly Vic and Leah were alone, looking into each other's eyes.

He reached out to brush strands of hair from her face. Leah forced herself not to lean into his touch, not to treasure those tingles. She looked away, and he dropped his hand.

"I probably never would stop fussing over you. Even if you were not hurt." She nodded at the ground. Leah did not dare look into those eyes. She feared she would see what she so desperately wanted to see—love, interest, commitment.

She was not ready.

Vic leaned forward, placed his hand on the wall behind her, and crossed his ankles. "Leah, I've been thinking . . . "

Footsteps sounded close by behind the wall.

"Vic? Leah? Javin says to call you two over for snacks before we . . . " Guy rounded the corner and came onto them. He stopped short. "Did I interrupt something?" His eyes flashed from Vic to Leah, as if trying to figure something out.

Vic casually pushed away from the wall and took a step back. "No, nothing at all. Lead us to the snack queen, messenger."

Guy shot them a strange glance before turning on his heels and heading over to the bench they'd dubbed—since that day Leah told them her vision—the *Bench of the Future*.

Leah's face warmed. Javin and Shana looked up as Guy, Vic, and Leah walked toward them.

Wordlessly, Javin handed her a plate of summer fruits and a glass of iced tea. "I would have offered these tempting pastries, but Vic warned me you'd refuse no matter how hard I try." Javin lifted the lid off a mini cooler to reveal an assortment of bite-sized cheesecakes.

"He was right." Leah grinned, giving the treats a sad look of farewell. "I suppose this tea is sweetened with honey?"

"Again, by Vic's insistence." Javin took a bite out of a chocolate mousse. "You don't know what you're missing out on."

"Processed white sugar, artificial flavors, GMO corn syrup, artificial color . . . " Leah counted off her fingers. "What else?"

Vic chuckled. "Visits to the doctor and heavy medical bills. Not to mention daily aches and pains." He caught Javin's eye and nodded in Leah's direction. "She has experience. Don't take my word for it."

Leah smiled at both of them. "Yep—the change in diet saved my mother's life. That, along with country living and God's mercy. And a couple of friendly, caring neighbors."

Shana grinned at Leah. "Especially the one who took the time to learn how to cook that way." She winked at her, then glanced at Vic.

"That, too." Leah tilted her head toward Vic, facing Javin. "So Jav, that's where I'm coming from on this. Because it changed my family's life. And I'm grateful for it."

"I'm convinced. It does make sense." Javin motioned for her to sit on the bench. "Take a seat. And don't feel awkward for sitting high up, you're our boss now. Vic. You come down and sit with us."

Vic complied, sitting on Leah's left while Javin sat on her right. Guy moved closer to Vic, so Shana was forced to sit beside Javin—which she did, after considerable complaining. Leah did not miss the small smile Shana gave Javin as he smirked at her and patted the ground beside him.

"How did we do, Leah?" Guy threw iced tea down his throat, looking sideways at her.

"From my perspective, you all did well. But I think I should be the one asking. What do you guys think? Is this doable?" She looked around, popping a strawberry into her mouth.

Javin swallowed the last of his dessert. "I need to work on clarifying and simplifying my descriptions of how exactly a move should be performed. This girl here—"

"My name is Shana, Javin." Shana raised an eyebrow at him.

"Miss Addams . . . "

"Shana."

"Miss Shana . . ."

"Shana!"

"*She* says that my verbal explanations were confusing and over-the-top." Javin nodded at Leah.

"He could demonstrate proper form and movement all right," Shana grudgingly conceded.

"Thank you, kind lady." Javin bent his head in her direction. "I'd say the same of you, but you haven't done your part yet."

"She will. Trust me. We'll have a couple more mock-training sessions like so—reaching into the more advanced moves—before we talk about kicking this off officially. Guy and Vic. Any complaints?"

"Guy is too smart for his own good. I've been telling him that all his life," Vic muttered, glaring at Guy.

Guy raised his eyebrows. "Maybe you're just having a hard time trying to keep up."

"I have to deal with you two on top of Jav and Shana?" Leah bit out, teasing.

"Hey, boss, conflict management training for you." Javin waggled his eyebrows and threw in a wink for good measure. Leah sighed.

"Practice makes perfect, eh? I guess I better get started. Guys, besides trading insults, do you have anything constructive to say about this training session?"

"Vic could improve on his confidence level. Toughen up and be more strict. I could learn from his patience."

"That's better. Vic?"

"I don't really have anything to add to that. I agree; I could be a little more strict." Vic waved at Guy's words.

Leah smiled and bit into a cube of cantaloupe. "Thanks for bringing us such a wonderful snack, Shana." Juice trickled out of the piece of fruit, and Leah gave it a little suck to prevent it from traveling to her chin.

"You're welcome."

"Did you just kiss the cantaloupe?" Vic's voice sounded strained. Leah looked at his completely serious eyes and began to choke. She brought her elbow to her mouth and coughed. Javin reached up and patted her on the back hard enough for the errant piece of fruit to slide back down the proper pipeline.

She gave Javin a grateful glance and tilted her head at Vic, eyebrows raised. "No. Why would I?"

Vic looked away, embarrassed. "I thought I heard you make a sound like you did, that's all." He cleared his throat loudly. "Forget I even said that."

"If you say that, I never will forget." Leah laughed and finished the rest of the fruit on her plate. As she got up to throw her plate away, her eyes locked with Vic's. He held her gaze in his for a couple of seconds. She tore her eyes away in time to notice Guy's thoughtful gaze on them. She shrugged at Guy.

"Let me get your plates." Javin held out a hand and gathered all five plates in one stack and their forks in another. "Shana, would you mind gathering the cups?"

"Javin, the plates are not disposable. I could reuse them . . . "

The two walked toward Shana's car, the cooler swinging between them. Silence descended onto the three friends who remained seated.

Leah's thoughts turned to Paul. Would Parkour be able to bring him out of the psychological and emotional chains binding him? "I'm not sure."

"Leah. Stop doubting God and start trusting in Him to lead you in the path He wants you to go." Leah did not realize she'd spoken out loud, but at Guy's serious tone, she turned and faced him, listening. "We've been praying together every week. I'm sure you pray about this all day long. And so far, the answer is yes."

"Guy's right, Leah. We're here. You have us and God. Stop listening to your doubts and fears—overcoming them is all this vision is about, eh?" Vic added, his eyes calming her heart.

Still, the memory surfaced. Overcoming obstacles—all except *that* one. The botched kong-gainer. The pain, the anger, the bitterness, the trauma. Fear and doubts? They were all there. Not going to overcome those anytime soon either.

Leah barked a laugh to hide her tension. "We all have something we could improve on, eh? Thanks for the encouragement, guys. I know I can depend on you."

"There's only one of me here." Guy pointed to himself. "This man is Vic. I'm Guy. Singular, male, and that's a proper noun."

Leah laughed. Vic joined in.

"What's the funny joke here?" Javin walked up to them, Shana not far behind.

"Never mind. Let's get back to work. We have a lot to do before we are ready to officially call ourselves Team Set Free to the world." Leah got to her feet, pushing herself up from the bench.

The four friends began to walk together a few steps ahead of her, back to the playground—their training complex. Vic looked back. "We're ready for it, girl set free."

CHAPTER TWELVE

The team decided to kick off on Canada Day, July first.

The five of them gathered in the park early Saturday morning and got to work setting up an information table, a table for snacks and refreshments, and chairs for people to sit around and enjoy each other's company. Shana pulled out a plastic banner and hung it over the blue "Information and Sign-up" gazebo Vic had just set up, stepping back to inspect her work.

"It's a wonderful day, eh? I can't believe we're actually doing this," Shana commented as she straightened the banner.

"It's been all work and no play the whole past month, girl," Guy grumbled at the huge speakers he was trying to connect to the laptop.

"That's not going to work, Guy. You need to find special adaptors for that. Try to plug in your iPod instead." Vic looked up from where he crouched on the ground, untying a red pop-up gazebo. Javin had managed to rent it from the softball group he was working with for the summer.

"You should design speakers to talk with your laptop, Vic," Guy muttered over his shoulder, turning to grab his phone and managed to knock into Javin.

"They're called wireless speakers, Guy. And stop complaining." Javin paused and wiped his forehead with his forearm. He moved the portable freezer to the edge of the refreshment table, opened it, and checked its contents. "Fruit platters, cheese and crackers. What's this, veggies? For Leah, I suppose. Ice cream with red maple leaf decorations . . . oh right, it's Canada Day."

"We know what's in there, Javin," Shana noted drily, spreading a cloth over the table in front of him. "Check the baked goods box and see if the pies are still in top condition. Someone could have driven more smoothly coming here."

Guy looked up with iPod in hand, triumphant. "It works fine, Vic. And Shana, next time you drive if you care so much for your dear pies."

Javin returned, carrying a box full of foil-covered circular plates. "Someone has to cut these up and serve them. They look all right to me. What flavor . . . what's this?" He pointed at something inside the box and began to read aloud. "To Leah, with kindest regards."

Shana leaned over, her eyes wide with interest. "That's not my handwriting. It's not one of my pies, either. See, it's done up differently from all the others."

"Good observation on top of fabulous cooking. You're a wonder, Shana." Javin's voice was warm. Shana looked at him, then ducked her head away.

Leah finished organizing the information table then lifted her head, propped a fist on her hip, and winked at Javin. "Paying compliments to my friend now, bro?"

Javin's face warmed, and he, too, ducked his head to hide a blush. "Hey, Leah. You got a secret admirer that sent you . . . hey, it's not here anymore!" He looked at Shana, at Guy, then narrowed his eyes at Vic, who was entirely focused on tying the last few cords of the gazebo cover around the top steel rods.

"Stop joking around, Javin. We have only half an hour until people start walking in." Leah pulled her laptop from the pile of bags and equipment under the refreshment table, powered up the computer, and pulled up the team website the five of them had created together. Guy had created an interactive and attractive theme that matched their team. She only hoped that the text she'd written—biographies, vision, mission statements, and such—would match the overall professional, passionate, and persuasive message. Then she headed over to their social media accounts, hoping to add a few pictures Shana had taken of themselves training together. Javin's indignant voice interrupted her train of thought.

"But I'm not! Your pie was here just now . . . I was wondering . . . " He searched vainly among the other pies.

"Javin, your long nights with the councilor trying to get one pitiful permit to use this place must have damaged your eyes somewhat. Let it go." Guy walked over, took the box out of his hand, and placed it on top of the waist-high cooler.

Shana turned toward them. "I saw it, too. And someone else was in the . . . "

"Look. Our first visitor." Vic pointed out with a rather relieved voice.

"What an unusual way to celebrate the birth of our country, friends." That smooth voice sent uncomfortable tingles down her back. Leah had a sense of foreboding as she turned to face the newcomer.

"Ethan. Good to see you again." She barely reined back her sarcasm. He'd better not try to mess things up.

"Leah. A pleasant surprise." He flashed a wide smile at her, his eyes darting daggers. Leah calmly stared back, daring him to speak. "I see you have been busy doing exactly what I've warned you against," he added, stepping closer to her and lowering his voice. Leah eyed him uneasily, then stepped back and headed over to the information table she'd vacated a few minutes ago.

"If you'll excuse us, Ethan. We still have a few things to work out before we can get the show rolling."

"Pitiful show that it is." His voice held a sneer.

That was too much. Leah took a deep breath and glared at Ethan. Barely keeping her voice level, she hissed, "What did you come for? To mess things up?"

He hissed back, eyes flashing. "What did you do this all for? To mess things up?"

Shana stepped up beside Leah as if to offer her support. Vic and Guy moved closer toward them from somewhere behind her.

"Shana, would you mind filling up the balloons over by the blue gazebo? Make sure that you all know your lines and moves for the show rotations." Leah waved her away, eyes on Ethan.

"Got it, boss," Javin answered for Shana, and the two of them moved off—but not before Shana gave her a side hug for encouragement and strength.

Vic shot her a confused and concerned look.

"I'll be fine," she mouthed, then walked over to the side with Ethan close behind. Once out of earshot from her team, she turned to him. "Ethan. This is not about you or about me, or even the team. It's about helping the teens and people of this community find freedom in life through Parkour. To find Christ."

"And you had to do that by doing what I especially warned you against." The intense blue eyes bored into hers. "Did you think you could come waltzing into this park, sign up a handful of kids, and ruin my business step-by-step?"

"That's not fair, Ethan." Leah tried her best to keep her voice calm—but it still shook. "I am not trying to ruin you. I . . . "

"That's exactly what you're doing," Ethan raised his voice, his lips twitching with annoyance.

"Ethan, I have to go. There are still a few things I need to touch up before people start coming in."

"Who would come to this pitiful little . . . ?"

Leah turned to go. "I'm sorry for whatever negative impact my team might have on you. Please accept my apologies. But know this— you could do nothing to stop us."

"Leah . . . " A vice-like hand landed on her shoulder, wrenching her off balance for a moment. Her weaker knee buckled under her, and she took an instinctive step back, landing against a well-developed chest.

Heat suffused her body—especially when she saw Vic making his way through the growing crowd toward her, eyebrows raised.

Ethan's arms went around her torso. "I'm just trying to get you to see reason. You would regret this."

"Is that a threat?" Leah tried to jab her elbows into Ethan's side, but her weak knee did not give her a proper stance to make much of an impact.

"Let. Me. Go." Leah gritted her teeth. The stress, anger, and over-powering embarrassment brought her near tears, but she was not going to break down. Not today.

Vic reached her side. "Let go of the lady." His voice was stern, calm, commanding. Ethan's body stiffened, and Leah could feel the intensity of their dueling stares. "Leave her—us—alone."

Ethan's hands left her body, and Leah immediately stepped out of their reach. He narrowed his eyes at her, breaking the staring contest between him and Victor.

"This conversation is not over yet." His voice was low and menacing. Leah stepped closer to Vic as if seeking shelter and strength. Vic placed an arm around her shoulder.

Ethan eyed them. "I'll leave you to your public event. Have a good day."

"We'll see you later, mister," Vic replied, his voice firm.

"You will." Ethan gave Leah a pointed glare, spun around, and strode quickly through the sparse crowd gathered in front of where Guy and Javin were busy cutting and handing out pies. Guy made eye contact with Vic and tilted his head toward the playground and brick wall. It was Vic's turn to give the seated audience a good show.

"You okay?" Vic gave her a squeeze, his eyes probing hers.

"I'm good." She gave him a reassuring smile, which did not reassure either of them. "Go and do your duty."

"As you wish, boss." He shot her a grin and trotted to "center stage"—the main playground.

He picked up the microphone lying on the closest stone with a flourish and addressed the fifty or so people assembled before him.

"Welcome, fellow Torontonians, to the first Parkour and freerunning demonstration by Team Set Free, a Parkour group dedicated to helping kids, young and old alike, overcome obstacles in life and live a fuller, happier life. My name is Victor, and I will be performing our first show to give you a taste of what we offer to teach. Please visit the information table during the break, and make sure to stay for the last and most spectacular show . . . "

The audience, which consisted of young families, high school teens, relaxing middle-aged couples, and active seniors, broke into applause. Leah clapped as Vic bowed to them, threw a backflip, and immediately began to freerun his way through the monkey-bars-and-rails obstacle course.

Leah watched Vic for a moment. Someone tapped her on the shoulder. She spun around. "Guy."

Guy gave her the briefest smile. "Your knee has not healed perfectly yet."

"How do you know?" Leah tried to hide her frustration with a smile.

Guy shrugged. "You're still limping a little. I could take over your demo for you. Man the information table for me in exchange."

"I'll be fine." Leah pursed her lips.

"I don't want you to hurt yourself trying to throw impressive moves in front of everybody." Guy stared her down. "Vic would never forgive me if I let you get hurt."

"All right." Leah let out a sigh of relief. "Thanks. Do me proud."

"I will." Guy walked away, sending her a glance over his shoulder and angling his head toward the information table. Leah took the cue, trotted over, and took her place beside Shana.

The young man and his mother walking up to her forced out smiles. Paul nodded a brisk hello and got down to business.

"My mom saw your team's ad in the *Toronto Star*." He nodded at the pamphlets and registration forms on the table between himself and Leah. "She thought it would be good for me to work with you guys."

Leah nodded and smiled at the forty-ish woman standing quietly beside her son.

"I'm not sure what good it would do, though. Nothing could . . ." He cut himself off mid-sentence and grew quiet. He looked away, his eyes hard and pained.

"Since his accident, he doesn't want to do anything. He's recovered as much as the doctors hoped, but he hadn't been the same person since then."

"Impossible when your dreams have been stolen from you forever, mom." His voice was one of a caged animal who'd given up. He looked from his mother to Leah. "Mom wanted to see if you could help me heal. On the inside."

Leah nodded. "We'll do our best to help you any way we can."

"I mean, Parkour's cool and all, but it's not going to help much."

"Give it a try, Paul." His mom patted his back. Paul sighed but picked up the pen and filled in the registration sheet.

The mother turned, her face carefully shielded. "Team Set Free is a religious group, aren't they? I heard some Christian music as your team members performed."

"Yes. We're a Christian group. Christ is a big part of what we do. Only God can heal the person from the inside out. We use Parkour as a channel to spread the Gospel and to lead others to healing and life through Him."

"Hmm." The woman's eyes narrowed, but she nodded. "We're not religious people, but I guess it's okay. It's just once a week, eh?" Leah nodded, tidying up scattered pamphlets.

"I guess your Jesus can't do my boy any harm." The woman checked Paul's registration form, signed the parental consent section, and handed the form to Leah. "We have to go now. I'm hoping your team can bring a smile back to my boy's face."

"Fat chance, mom." He gave a single wave to Leah as he turned to leave.

"See you next week!" She turned to Shana, who wiped a bead of sweat from her forehead before giving Leah a tired smile.

"That would be our seventh sign up. And we still have half an hour before we're officially done for the day."

"That's great news, Shana." Leah sat down on the folding chair behind her, reaching for a water bottle. "I feel somewhat faint. Take over for me for a bit, Shana?"

"No problem, Leah." Shana moved to the middle of the information table as a girl and her mother stepped closer.

"Hi, I'm Shelley McGyver, and this is my girl Minnie. She is fourteen years old . . . "

A tap on her shoulder took her attention away from the visitors. A smiling Vic held out a generous slice of blueberry pie, along with a glass of apple juice. "You've been working yourself to death. Feeling faint is absolutely normal. Here, have a bite. And before you ask, it's gluten-free." He winked and passed her the plate.

"Looks tempting. Thanks for being so thoughtful, Vic." Leah took a bite and smiled. "Tastes wonderful."

"I told you she'd like it, Vic. No need to worry." Shana commented, turning toward them as Minnie filled out the sheet with her mom's help. "Leah, I'll have you know my cousin spent an hour making that pie."

Leah looked up, surprised. "You made this. For me?"

Vic nodded, his face flushed. Or was it from the runs he had performed? That was fifteen minutes ago.

Leah stared into the thinning crowd, her eyes looking back into the past. Every week, Shana and Vic would knock on their door, arms full of wholesome food, wide smiles on their faces. They were her dearest friends during that time—but things were different now. Weren't they? Did this gift signify something more—or did he just make this for her knowing that she'd miss the "normal" pies Shana made?

"I'm sorry I embarrassed you," Vic spoke after a while. He touched her chin, forcing her to face him. "But pink does look good on you." Leah caught her breath, choked, and turned her head away to cough into the crook of her elbow.

When she could talk again, she faced Vic and lifted an eyebrow. "What was that?"

"Stop teasing her, Vic," Shana interposed, then turned on Leah with a twinkle in her eyes. "He could be sweet if he wants to, eh, Leah?"

"Shana." Leah murmured in a warning voice, then turned to Vic standing beside her. "Vic, this is so sweet of you. Reminds me of the good times we had in the past."

Vic shook his head, glancing away. "Leah, this has nothing to do with the past. I remember what happened. But if you could only look beyond that and see what I . . . " He paused, looked at her with troubled eyes, and looked away again.

Leah waited for him to finish his thought: when he didn't, she spoke up. "I did not get a chance to thank you for helping me out earlier this morning when Ethan."

Vic nodded. "It's okay, Leah."

Shana turned back to her duties.

"You came just in time." Leah took another bite of the pie.

Vic shifted in his seat. "Did you know him? Was he one of your . . . ?"

"Yes, we've met before." Leah wondered why he sounded so uncomfortable.

"No, I mean . . . was he someone special?" Vic avoided her eyes. "Shana mentioned . . . "

"You trust your cousin?" Leah smirked. "But to answer your question, no. Though I think he wants me to think of him that way." She paused and took a bite of pie.

"Good to know."

Leah lifted an eyebrow at him. Vic shrugged. Leah let the comment drop and concentrated on the pie.

"What did he want to talk to you about?" Vic lowered himself onto a camping chair nearby. Leah thought for a moment. Should she brush it aside? It was not serious. It wouldn't do to worry her team so soon. "It's nothing, Vic. He just wanted to continue a conversation we had when we first . . . "

"Are we talking about the blond-haired flirt?" Guy had finished cleaning the snack table.

Vic looked between Guy and Leah. "Flirt? What do you mean?" Vic turned to Leah. "Should I be concerned?"

"Vic. I'm not interested in him at all."

"It's getting on my nerves." Vic jumped up from the camping chair he'd been sitting on. "I'll pack up the sound system. Help Javin take down the gazebos."

"Interesting." Guy murmured as Vic left. "I thought he wouldn't care so much. Maybe . . . " Guy let his sentence hang.

"Guy, stop hinting at . . . whatever you're hinting at. He didn't mean anything by it." Leah got up and turned away.

"Leah? Lost in thought? Want to help me take these to the car?" Javin waved at her, motioning to the cooler and empty aluminum pie pans.

"Sure, no problem." Leah bent and pulled at one of the handles of the cooler. "I could take those cardboard boxes, too."

"I got it." Javin balanced the pile of empty containers on his head and took up the other handle of the cooler.

"Nice turnout, eh? The weather was perfect."

"Thank God for that." Leah walked in step with Javin to Shana's sedan, parked near the curb in front of the park. "We have about ten kids signed up. Classes start next week, Tuesday night."

"That's great. Today was great." Javin flashed her a smile as he hefted the cardboard boxes into the trunk of the car.

Leah nodded. She adjusted the box of utensils and empty pie dishes and plates in the trunk then stood back up again. "Thanks for being part of this, for making this possible, for doing your part."

"Pass that on to the rest of the team—they all deserve some praise and encouragement."

"I cannot wait for the first class to begin next week." Leah smiled.

Javin looked at her, his lips curling. "Same here, boss."

CHAPTER THIRTEEN

A family—a girl and a boy who looked alike, and a woman—strode up to her. Leah smiled. The three thunderclouds of faces stared back. Leah felt uncomfortable but brushed her feelings aside and greeted them.

"Hello, and welcome. Are you guys here for the Parkour training class?"

The woman nodded, not making eye contact. She released her grip on the two children and got to business.

"This is Andrea and her brother, Owen." The thirty-ish woman tightened her lips and pushed the two look-alike fourteen-year-olds toward Leah. "I'll be back to pick them up in an hour. That's how long the class is, right?"

"Yes, ma'am. You're welcome to stay and enjoy the park if you like." Leah smiled at the two teens. No response.

"I have a meeting with my lawyer. I'll see you later." The woman snatched her purse, whipped out a couple of bills, and yanked them toward Leah. "That should be enough." Before Leah could thank her, the woman spun around and fast-walked to the van she'd just exited.

The girl looked up at Leah, her face hard. "My parents are getting a divorce. They hate each other. My brother and I hate each other. What are you going to do about that?" She crossed her arms.

Leah did her best to smile. "First, we'll warm up with stretches and a run around the park. We'll chat a little, get to know each other. Maybe you could make friends with the other kids as well. Then we're going to teach you all the basics of Parkour movement."

"You going to teach me how to flip?" Owen turned toward her, a hint of interest in his sullen eyes.

Leah smiled. "Not today. But we'll get there."

"Huh. Thought so." Owen forced a laugh. He glanced at Javin leading Paul and Minnie into basic stretches. "What if I don't want to do this?"

"You don't have a choice." Leah began to walk toward the group.

"That's what my mom always tells us. She forced us to come here—she doesn't even have time for her own kids." The anger in Andrea's voice did not hide the hurt the teen was going through. Leah paused and turned to them.

"Owen and Andrea. We're all here to learn and grow. I know that you guys are going through a hard time, but while here, you are going to cooperate and learn how to do Parkour. We respect each other and refrain from bad-mouthing our lives or people. Understood?"

The twins stared at her, nodding.

"Good. Now join those kids and stretch your way to a positive attitude."

"As if." Owen huffed, scowling. But the twins moved in that direction and copied the stretches Javin demonstrated.

A few more kids joined them as their parents dropped them off, some staying behind to watch on the benches or walk around the park. Most teens were between the ages of thirteen and sixteen, with the exception of Paul and shy Gina, both seventeen.

As Vic led the kids onto the rubber jogging track that ran around half the park, Leah counted thirteen kids total. She fell in line behind them, noticing the kids making small talk with Vic, who yelled out encouragements every now and then. Leah gave Vic a thumbs up when she caught his eye. Things were going as planned. So far, so good.

After the run, Leah took Gina and Minnie to the monkey bars. The rest of the kids were working with the four other Team Set Free members, each working in a different section of the park and training with whatever their environment offered.

Leah glanced at the strikingly different girls entrusted to her charge. Minnie wore clothes that were a few sizes too small for her, emphasizing her round stomach. Her shoes and graphic tee screamed orange and pink, which almost hurt to look at in the bright sun. Blonde hair, blue eyes, and pouty faced, Minnie was the polar opposite of the quiet, slender girl who stood painfully shy to the side, her face hidden by the curly hair loosely tied into a ponytail behind her. Gina reached taller than Leah's 5'5," but the combination of loose clothing that hung off her bony shoulders, and her slouching posture, brought her to Leah's height.

Leah smiled at them, trying to make eye contact. "We're going to practice monkey bars. Later on we're going to teach you how to perform bar laches, which I'll show you in a minute. But first, I want you two to take turns doing this."

Leah walked under the first bar, jumped, gripped the metal bar, and hung on. "Pull yourself across using your arms. We need to work on our arm muscles. Go all the way across." She demonstrated. "Then we're going to speed things up a little. Like this." Leah came back—hand after hand—quicker than the first pass.

"Okay. Who would like to give it a try?"

Gina, who'd been watching Leah's moves out of the corner of her eye, looked around carefully, then lifted her hand. Leah gave her a smile.

"Good for you, Gina. Let's hop onto the bars and get moving. Minnie, come over and get ready. You're going to go two bars behind her."

Minnie nodded nervously, fumbling toward the step up to the bars. She lifted one neon pink sneaker and pulled herself up with a grunt.

Gina gave the first bar a wary glance, reached a hesitant hand, and touched the bar. "It will hold you up, Gina. Grip it with both hands. You've probably done this in school, too, right?"

Gina nodded slowly. "I'm not good at it," but she reached up her other hand, held firm, and let her legs hang.

"Reach for the next bar—that's it. Keep going." Leah encouraged, as Gina made her way from one bar to the next.

Leah made sure Gina was doing okay before trotting back to where Minnie was still struggling to reach the first bar.

"Jump up a little, Minnie. It's only a few inches."

"I'm going to fall on my face if I miss, and that girl's going to laugh at me." Minnie wiped at her eyes and sniffled.

Leah sighed. "Girl, no one will laugh at you. Don't worry. Jump and trust your hands to hold tight to the bar. You'll do fine."

Minnie looked up at the bar, then at Leah, who stood at eye level with her on the ground. "When I do this at school, the other kids laugh at how slow or fat I look. See, Gina's already finished." Minnie pointed to the other end of the bars.

"That's your cue to go, girl." Leah ignored her complaints and instead focused on the here and now. "You can do this. Be confident. You said you've done this before?"

"Yes." Minnie sniffed. She reached vainly for the bar, then sighed. "Okay, I'm going to jump, even if my shirt flies up when I'm at it."

Leah smiled in encouragement. "Think about what you're going to do, not what people think about you. You really can't change or help what others think. Just do your best. I'll be here to help if you need it."

Reach by slow reach, Minnie made her way to the other side. The two girls smiled at each other. "Gina. Go back a little faster this time, okay?"

"Yes, Miss Leah." The girl whispered before reaching for the first bar and swinging across. She smiled shyly at Leah as she passed her: a voluntary grin that Leah returned.

Fifteen minutes later, the girls were ready to move on to precision jumps. Leah led them over to where Vic was coaching a few boys on how to land a jump properly—with the balls of the feet absorbing most of the impact and body leaning slightly forward, knees bent.

They looked up as Leah and the two girls approached.

"Vic, could you tell me where you got those twigs from?" Leah pointed to the sticks on the ground around his feet. "They're perfect training tools."

"Here, you take these." He handed her a couple of the straightest sticks. "You got the smallest group, lucky you." He smiled at Leah and waved at the girls. "Enjoying it so far?"

Gina nodded, her eyes darting from Vic to Paul, who'd come around from behind one of the other boys and was now staring intently at Gina, mesmerized by this slip of a girl. They exchanged shy smiles, and Paul nodded to her as if they knew each other. Gina held her head higher. Paul's face was momentarily transformed—as if new life had come into him.

Minnie's whining voice interrupted Leah's thoughts.

"My arms are hurting from all that hanging and swinging."

Vic smiled. "That's normal. Let's help your legs hurt so that you're balanced out. Then we'll give your abs a workout so you'll hurt all over."

They all laughed. Leah took the offered sticks and set them up about three feet apart a few paces beside the boy's group.

"Okay. Here's where things start to get more interesting. You guys are going to do this." Leah stepped on a twig, bent her knees into a squat-like position, and swung her arms forward. "Then you're going to jump, and land like this . . . "

She suited her actions to her words.

" . . . And land on this twig on the balls of your feet. Like so." Leah exaggerated her heel *not* touching the ground during her landing. "Got it?"

The two girls nodded. "Why don't you go first this time, Minnie?"

Minnie shook her head. "I'm too heavy. I can't jump that far."

Leah was silent for a while. "Minnie. Look at me." She waited for the teen to meet her eyes. "Do not ever use your weight or height as an excuse not to do something. You are stronger and more capable than you think. I do not want to hear you talk down about yourself again, okay?" Leah cut her eyes at Gina. She was biting her nails, her eyes wide with understanding.

Minnie nodded. "I'm sorry."

"You did nothing wrong, girl. Just let go of your insecurities and go for the jump. It's safe, and it's not impossible. Now get on the stick and get into position."

"Okay. Like this?" Minnie's voice was hopeful. She bent her knees, lifting her arms.

"You're bending over too much. Straighten your back. You're going to swing your arms later, right when you're lifting off." Minnie adjusted her form. "That's it. Now push off from the ground, and swing your arms out in front of you at the same time. Don't lean too far forward, or else you're going to land too soon."

Minnie nodded, pressed her lips together in concentration, and jumped, landing a few inches short of the stick.

"Try again, Minnie. Pretend this stick is the top edge of a wall, like that one." She pointed to the concrete wall a yard away. "You want your feet to land securely on the stick. Jump as if the distance here between the sticks is really a drop—in other words, if you miss it, you're going to fall. Try that."

Leah gave her a pat on the back, then moved over and set up two more sticks for Gina. 'Do the same thing here. Land on the other stick with the balls of your feet. Get into position . . . "

The team stood together and waved as the last student crawled into his parent's van, and the car roared away. The sun cast a soft reddish hue on them and on the now-quiet park.

"This knee would be as good as new in no time, giving it this gentle exercise I just did," Leah commented, flexing her knee a few times before lowering herself to the ground. Vic gripped her elbow and helped her down the last, hardest few inches. "Thanks."

"It's amazing how tiring one session can be, and I'm not even moving that much." Shana took a long swallow from her water bottle, tilting her head back and letting her ponytail sweep the ground. "I'm all sweaty now."

Javin was looking at her with open admiration, rubbing a hand over his mouth and mustache. "You look perfect sweaty or not," he said softly.

Shana sat back upright, sputtering, her face red. "What did you say . . . ? No, wait. I heard that. Uh . . . thanks, I guess."

"Too tired to shoot him down?" Guy crossed his legs and sat beside Shana.

Shana shrugged. She shot Javin an embarrassed glance, then looked at Leah. "It was a blast teaching these kids."

"They could be a handful at times." Vic chewed a protein bar. "Paul was in my group. He had some trouble doing the handstands due to complications with his spine from an accident. All the other boys in the class taunted him, and he mowed them down, verbally and physically. I had a rough time bringing things back into order."

"Told you to be more strict, especially with teenage boys." Guy took a swig of water.

"Whatever. Things went smoother after I explained that we're all here to learn, and there would be no bad-mouthing each other because of whatever problems we have." Vic concluded and turned to Leah.

Leah nodded. "Setting down a couple of ground rules and keeping them is something we'll have to work on, definitely. I had a girl who talked herself into not being able to do something she really was able to."

"Guy? How were your boys and girls?" Javin prompted, after a moment of silence.

"No one wants to cooperate with either me or each other. They'd stand as far apart as possible—still within earshot, and give only nods or one-word answers whenever I asked something, or whenever some kid tried to initiate conversation, which was pretty rare." He paused. "You know those two twins who came late? They were pretty much enemies. Didn't speak a word. Shoved each other all the time. They treated the other kids better, but still." Guy blew out a frustrated breath. "Everyone was happy to have the session over with."

"My group won't stop talking long enough for me to get a word in," Shana spoke. "I had two girls and one boy, and they were giggling and teasing each other all over the place. I had to be quite stern to get anything in between their joking around."

"Maybe we should mix the kids every other session? Help them get to know each other, work with different people, learn from each other." Leah leaned on her elbows, looking around at the team.

"If it won't be too confusing to the kids and ourselves then, yes, I think it's a great idea," Javin said.

Vic crumpled the bar-wrapper in his hand and stuffed it into his shorts pocket. "We need a hundred percent-perfect moves for the kids to get promoted to another level, eh? I know we have a chart where you've listed out the specific moves for each level, but does each move have to be totally perfect before we move on?"

"What if you missed a precision by ten percent, Vic? What do you think would happen?" Guy shook his head as if he could not believe how easy Vic could be on the kids. Guy looked at Leah and shrugged. "Maybe I'm too strict."

"You have a good point, Guy. Vic, I think that proper form and control are absolute musts when it comes to movement as a whole. But when it boils down to specific moves . . . we all have things we are still working on and improving. This is what I think: make sure the kid is on an upward trajectory, improvement-wise, before moving on. Besides that, I'd say it's a case-by-case basis. Each person is different, each approach is different . . . there's not much I could say."

Vic nodded. "Okay."

Leah looked at the sun. It was sinking toward the horizon. "It's late. You guys can go on home, or wherever. I'll stay here a bit to plan out the next training, dream, and watch the sun set over downtown Toronto."

"Sounds like a plan," Vic said. He stretched himself out on the bench, the soles of his feet resting against Guy's elbow. "Wake me when you're ready to leave."

"Go home and sleep, Vic." Guy poked him on the thigh.

"Who says? I'm just tired." Vic yawned to prove his point.

Shana lowered herself to the ground to Leah's right without a word, her eyes glued onto the bluish pink clouds gracing the sky over the setting sun. Her shoulders drooped with exhaustion.

"So are we all." Javin looked at Shana, then followed her line of vision to the sky above.

They were silent for a few minutes, lost in their own thoughts.

Leah broke the silence, bringing her knees up to her chin. "I wonder if I could do any more to help them. Help them find faith in God? Know that He's their only Rock and Anchor when all else fails? I'm far from perfect, but those kids look up to us as examples. Mentors. People they could trust. What if . . . I don't measure up?"

Her question hung like an ominous cloud above them. No one spoke. No one answered. Leah took in a deep breath and exhaled. Two tears fell.

Guy shifted and sat closer to Leah, staring into her eyes. "Leah. I'm not sure if anyone could answer that fully and correctly. And I know you've heard all the clichés people could and do say—none of us are perfect, we learn from each other, God opens hearts, and so on. But, I have something that could help you.

"My parents divorced when I was less than a year old. My mother married another guy. We moved in with this stepdad, and life as a family began. Dad claimed to be a Christian. He had his rough spots, which made for some rather uncomfortable moments in our family life. I . . . I'd look at him and think, 'Can a guy live like this and call himself a Christian?' I was angry. My mom would cry in the night. We begged him to change. Then one night, we found out he was living another life in another province where he worked for weeks at a time as a truck driver. Another woman. Another family. We were devastated, to say the least. One night . . . his truck went out of control. Spun off the highway. He was in a coma when we saw him at the hospital.

"He was near death. I didn't know how much I loved this guy until he was about to die." Guy choked. "He woke up one day, but he was so near death it was like he could drift away anytime. He called my mom and myself over to his bedside and told us he'd lived a double life and was sorry for it. He asked my mom and me to forgive him and learn this one important lesson. He told me I can never trust myself or other people too much. We're all imperfect. But we know One who is perfect in all ways, and it's our duty to point others to Him.

In our weakness, His strength is made manifest. He said, 'I know I've been a bad example to you. I want to point you to God. He's the one person Who'd never fail you. Trust Him. He'll never let you down.'"

Guy's voice broke for a second. When he spoke again, his voice was soft. "That's what I have to say to you, Leah. Trust God. Not us. Not yourself."

"Guy's right, Leah. Stop doubting yourself and start trusting God. Point to God when we slip and miss the mark." Shana's eyes held Leah's for one, long minute.

Leah nodded, her eyes filling with another kind of tears altogether. Wiping them away, she laughed at herself. "Thanks." She looked at Javin and Guy. "Thanks for the encouragement. I'm blessed to have friends like you guys." She looked around. The sun was more than half gone.

"It's time to head back."

CHAPTER FOURTEEN

"You'll take Owen, Andrea, Paul and . . ." Javin's voice drifted off as he pointed out the kids to Leah. Victor, standing in the middle of a growing group of young adults, was waving Leah over.

"Sorry, Jav. I'll see what Vic is up to." Leah trotted over to where Vic was standing beside a Chinese couple and their a sixteen-year-old girl. All of them looked uncomfortable and downcast, but their faces brightened up when Leah stepped up beside Vic.

Vic gestured at the small family, his eyes pleading with hers. "I can't exactly communicate in Chinese . . ."

"Be glad to, Vic." Leah smiled at the newcomers and said hello in both Cantonese and Mandarin.

The mother smiled and broke into a long string of Mandarin. Being Cantonese by birth, it took Leah a moment to absorb what the woman was saying.

"My daughter wants to learn, but she is afraid. We have just emigrated from mainland China, and she has no friends here. We want to help her find friends and learn some English because we—" she pointed to herself and her husband—"we do not speak good English. Can you help us?"

Leah nodded. Replying in Mandarin, she explained how the classes work and what the girl would have to do in order to be part of a group.

"We have money. We can pay." The husband dug out a wallet. "How much?"

He handed over the amount. The mother motioned at the girl, who looked less worried now. Chinese immigration to the Greater Toronto Area was a growing trend the last couple of years, yet they were hard-pressed to find friends.

The mother pointed at her daughter. "Very obedient girl." She said in broken English as if hoping that she could persuade Leah.

"That is a blessing. Thank you so much for bringing her to us." Leah switched back to Mandarin and outlined how the class would work this afternoon.

After the couple left, Leah smiled and made small talk with the girl as they strolled to join the others. Her name was Ashlee, and she preferred to communicate in Mandarin.

Today would be an interesting challenge. Just one more obstacle to a smoothly-run day.

"It's been three months. When do we start training flips?" Owen crossed his hands and stared at Leah.

Andrea stepped on her brother's toes. "Shut your big mouth, Wannabe."

"Oh yeah? Who's older here, Miss Wannabe?"

Goodness. They were sparring with their shared last name now. "Owen. Andrea. Cut it out." Leah waited until the two kids were focused on her instead of glaring at each other. "We'll be training flips indoors at the gym down the street. But you've got to be able to reach level three before you can do that."

"Sheesh. You are too hard on us."

"Don't play that card on me, Owen." Already forty minutes had passed. With four kids on her hands, each at a different level of progress—and with a thread of anger and bitterness running through the entire team—she felt ready to snap at everyone.

"You might as well take the test now, smarty-pants," Paul spoke up from his supine position on top of the concrete slab he was practicing precisions on minutes ago.

"Paul, no name-calling here." Leah motioned toward the walls. "Your precisions look good. Start training the crane after you've jumped that large gap perfectly twenty times." Leah pointed at a five-foot gap between two brick walls.

Paul got up with a grimace. "My back is hurting again. I don't feel like doing this."

"Paul. Is it too painful for you to go for it? Or is it just muscle pain?" Leah tilted her head.

"It's . . . it's not from my injury. I think it's just because you've been working us too hard." He scowled at Leah.

"Paul. If it's just muscle pain, you have to push through it. This class will last for only about fifteen more minutes. You can rest after that."

Paul sighed, but headed toward the one wall, climbed on top, and practiced the crane position—one leg reaching down the wall, the other foot perched on the top of the wall, the same leg bent at the knee, his two hands gripping the wall and holding his body in place—before standing on top and looking critically at the opposing wall. He narrowed his eyes with determination. And leapt.

Was it just hopefulness on her part, or was Paul's face actually happier than on his first day? Healing takes time, but it was happening. Paul landed solidly, jumped at the other wall, and landed in a crane position. He looked at Leah and smiled. A real, uninhibited smile. She felt her own face reciprocate as her heart lifted.

That was one kid on his way to restoration.

Leah turned to Owen and Andrea, who were engaged in a hard-core sibling-shoving fight. The girl had guts. Owen was significantly larger than she was, but she held her ground. Impressive, but this fight was not right.

"Guys, stop. Owen, you have ten minutes to show me what you've got for the level three test. Same for you, Andrea. Or else you're both going to practice precisions with Paul."

Andrea pouted.

"This is not a baby event or a kid's Parkour training class. We're treating you like adults here. Toughen up and make a decision. Test or precisions?"

Andrea looked at Owen, who was sprawled on the ground by now, and turned to Paul, who executed the crane-like precision landing again and again.

"That." Andrea pointed at Paul. "I want you to teach me that."

"Sorry, Andrea: not the crane. Your precisions are not solid enough. Maybe next time. Head over there and see if you can jump as far as Paul there." The girl shuffled away, her forehead creased and face annoyed.

"I'll do the test." Owen squinted at her, his body stretched out on the grass.

"Get off the ground, big boy. You're almost fifteen years old." Leah waited for Owen to stand before continuing. "You have three tries at the test: this will be your second. It's everything from level one to level two, on top of the level three stuff."

"Come on. I'm tired. Take it easy on me."

"Parkour—life in general, really—won't go easy on you if you're tired or sad or whatever. You've got to do what you've got to no matter what you feel. Now get up and show me a proper Parkour roll from the ground."

"Not that baby move." Owen's whiny voice grated on Leah's nerves. She turned away. "Owen, whenever you decide to grow up and act on your own decisions, come over. I'll be teaching Ashlee over here."

"Personal responsibility is key," Leah muttered to herself as she headed to the silent girl hanging around and watching Vic with wide eyes. Leah paused as Vic bounded like a monkey toward them. His infectious smile brightened her stressful day.

"Why the long face, boss?" He teased as he landed on the rock she leaned against.

"Long . . . face?" Ashlee squinted at Leah, then at Vic. "She has . . . long face?"

Leah smiled. "He means I look a little sad or stressed out. Unhappy," Leah clarified. She turned to Vic. "What about you? Don't you have your own kids to teach?"

"Nope. I told Guy to take over for me when he commented that you seemed to have a certain gentleman who might need a little reprimanding." He looked around, then stared at Gina, who stood close to Paul, looking up at him with open admiration in his eyes. They seemed to be making small, though intense, talk. "Gina's in my group, but somehow she got away as I was transferring my kids over into Guy's hands. I hope you're okay with them talking and training together for a while as I help you out?"

Leah watched the interaction between the two teens, a wistful smile on her face. "I think they had a crush on each other." Paul reached down, grasped Gina's two upstretched arms, and pulled her up beside him. Gina's smile was bolder than Leah had ever seen from her.

Vic turned to the two teens just in time to catch Paul tilting Gina's chin toward him as he said something in a low tone. "Should we be concerned?"

"It's just a crush. Maybe it would be best to keep an eye on them if anything gets out of hand. No pun intended."

Vic nodded. And sighed. "Crushes in high-school years are normal. We all had them. People we dreamed of, and never got a chance to . . . " He cut himself off mid-sentence and turned to her, eyes blank of whatever emotion was in his voice. "The boy I came for?"

Leah tore her thoughts away from Paul and Gina—and Vic's cryptic statements—and pointed at Owen. "Owen there. He might need some tough coaching, though."

"I've learned a few things along the way." Vic brushed the reminder aside lightly and hopped over to where Owen was sitting on the grass and covering his shorts with what wilted vegetation he'd been gleaning from the ground. "Hey buddy, get up and start moving along. What level are you working on?"

"That strict ninny over there told me to do a lousy roll for her."

Leah bent down and set up the two precision trainers Javin had made with a couple of two-by-fours and some screws last week. "Here, Ashlee. Step on this board and jump onto the other one." She repeated herself in Mandarin to make sure the girl understood. Vic's voice caught her attention.

"That ninny over there is right. Show me." Leah heard the smirk in his voice and bristled, even though she knew Vic was just playing along.

"Did you just call me a ninny, Vic?"

Vic ignored her, but she could see his body shaking with suppressed laughter. She glared at his back.

"Care to elaborate on why exactly you chose to encourage him to call me that?"

She did her best to keep her voice in check, but a yelling tone came into her voice nonetheless, along with a healthy touch of angry annoyance. Ashlee looked up with surprise and apprehension. "You . . . angry?"

There goes her being a good example. She nodded at Ashlee, guilt and shame filling her heart. "I'm sorry, Ashlee." Guy's message to her three months ago resurfaced in her mind. She swallowed and prayed for wisdom.

Owen was still whining his way through his 'test.' Leah guessed he'd not even gone through the level one recap. She sighed and motioned for Ashlee to jump again.

Someone tapped her on the shoulder. "Leah, I want to apologize for calling you a ninny." Vic's face was contrite.

Leah nodded. "Go ahead."

"Huh?" Vic's face was confused.

Ashlee's head tilted, her eyes shifting from one to another. Out of the corner of her eye, Leah saw Andrea climb down from the slab she was on, walk up to Owen, and copy his posture—arms crossed, glowering at Vic and Leah.

"When are you going to test me on the special tricks and stuff, Vic?" Owen shoved Andrea with his elbow—she returned the favor, sticking her tongue out at him.

"Guys. Stop that now." Vic spoke without taking his eyes off Leah. "This is more important than the pseudo test you were taking."

"Come on, my mom paid for this." Owen's voice lost its brashness and defiance.

"What do you mean, Leah?" Vic ignored Owen's half-hearted jab. "I just apologized."

"You asked me for permission to do so, and I gave you the go ahead. Finish the job you started, old man." Leah smirked, lifting an eyebrow, challenging him.

"I'm sorry I called you a ninny, Leah." Vic held out his hand with a repentant smile. "I was wrong to do that. Forgive me?"

Leah smiled, her heart warming from the look in Vic's eyes. "Apology accepted, Vic. I forgive you." They shook hands, Vic holding on to her hand a second longer than necessary. Their gazes locked for one long second. Leah was the first to look away.

"I wish my parents did that more often. They don't even talk to each other anymore." Owen's voice was barely above a whisper. There was hurt and raw pain in his previously defiant and rebellious tone. "They never apologize to each other. If they'd done that . . . what you two just did . . . maybe things won't be as bad as they are now."

Leah's throat constricted. Was this the door Guy noted God might open? She exchanged a surprised, yet hopeful look with Vic, then turned to Owen.

Before she could say anything, though, Andrea sniffed and wiped at her eyes. "My dad and mom call each other bad names all the time. They yell and fight. I've never seen them say anything nice to each other. I hope they'd just be nice to each other and forgive each other, like you and Mister Vic just did. Shake hands, say you're sorry and all that."

"It takes a good dose of humility and love to do that. And a willingness to forgive and forget the wrong the other person did to you." Paul's serious voice broke into the conversation. He sat off to the side, his thin arms around his knees, his eyes looking out past the group, past the present, back to a hurt-filled past. Gina sat beside him, leaning into his side. "I never truly forgave the person who cut all my dreams to pieces."

"What happened?" Ashlee's wide eyes stared at Paul.

He looked at her briefly, his eyes shadowed by pain-filled memories. The hard lines around his mouth creased. "I was biking. Living my dream, preparing for a big competition I was looking forward to. A guy in front of me opened his car door, and I smashed into it. I flew off my bike, landed on a car, slid off the car, and fell onto the street."

"Oh no!" Andrea caught her breath, her hand covering her mouth. "Did you break your spine?"

"No, but that guy's stupid move killed my dreams. The doc said I could never be a triathlon again—complications with how the injury had recovered since or something. I mean, sure I could exercise. Heck, I'm doing Parkour. But never run, swim, and bike competitively. That dream's gone." His voice broke. "I keep thinking if only that guy had looked before he opened his door, if only he'd closed it after I blew my bike horn . . . if only he'd done what he should have done, I would be where I'd dreamed I would be. Not here trying to live life like a normal kid again." He dropped his head, a glimmer of moisture between those dark lashes.

Leah let a few silent minutes pass. Then she quietly said to everyone present, "My mother told me that in God's world there are no 'what if's.' There's no 'if only's.' There's nothing we can do to change the past. The only thing we could do is to live despite it in order to be the people God wants us to be, by His grace. We're not perfect. None of us are. Paul, I know it's hard to forgive to the man who crippled you from your dreams, but know this: you're not doing anyone a favor by holding this against him. And you're not that much better than he is. We're all sinners. We've all done things that were wrong."

"Like when I take mama's money to buy candy?" Ashlee interrupted.

"Or like when my mom snuck out to make out with another man while my dad wasn't around?" Owen muttered bitterly.

"Or the time I pushed a girl down because she was calling me bad names and laughing at my clothes." Andrea stared at her feet.

"None of us are perfect, but there is Someone Who loves us no matter what we've done," Vic said. "Jesus Christ died for all of us, for the wrongdoings we've committed, so that we could live redeemed lives through Him and live together with Him in heaven."

"My friends say that's all a bunch of fairy tales. You guys believe that stuff?" Defiance crept back into Owen's voice.

Leah looked him in the eye. "Yes, I do. God has changed me from the inside out, and I believe He can change us all for His glory, if we let Him. He could help you love your parents. Paul, God can help lift that burden from you and help you forgive the man for harming you."

Paul nodded. "This is all new to me, but I'll think about it. How did you know it was a burden though . . . " he mused as he got up and went back to the walls.

Owen looked at Leah with disbelief. "I don't know if your God could really help my parents."

"We don't know how to pray, Miss Leah." Andrea interrupted, her voice subdued. "Could you pray for us, for our mom and dad? That they could be nice to each other, like Vic was with you?"

Leah nodded, her eyes filling. "We'd love to, Andrea."

Owen was blinking furiously. "I'm going to train a little harder now. I thought you all were just about fun and games, but now you guys make me into a soggy mess. If your Jesus could change my family . . . " He stomped off, frustrated at his own tears. Andrea nodded at Leah and followed her brother to the grass, where they leap-frogged over each other as a training for the Kong vault.

"They're getting along, eh?" Vic stuck his hands into his pockets.

Leah turned to him, her eyes shining. "Yes. I pray we're making a real difference in their lives."

"I think you're right, Leah." He paused and turned to Owen and Andrea, walking over to teach them some more. "But you were wrong about one thing."

"And what is that, pray tell?" Leah crouched, adjusted Ashlee's precision trainers, and grinned up at Vic.

His eyes were warm as he smiled at her over his shoulder. "I'm not an old man yet."

CHAPTER FIFTEEN

Leah parked her Jeep at the Vault. With her mp3 player and a pair of earbuds in hand, she exited her car, locking the door behind her. She smiled to herself as she turned and jogged down the sidewalk toward "their" park.

She was back to her freerunning training—on everything, that is, except the kong-gainer. She was not touching that. Pain flashed through her mind, the old fear overcoming her. She closed her eyes and took a deep, stabilizing breath.

She put on her favorite workout playlist, stuck her earbuds into her ears, and stretched to the rhythm of the songs from the mp3 clipped to her yoga pants.

The park was deserted and empty, the swings swinging back and forth in the breeze. Just perfect for a semi-private training session.

She leaped onto the wall before her, muscled-up, and vaulted over the haphazardly placed brick wall segments some creative park designer had planned for the park.

Reaching the concrete slabs, she transitioned to bounding and precision jumping, allowing herself to smile and feel the energy pulsing through her body. The uneven surface scraped along the soles of her freerunners, the sounds of her feet making contact with the concrete muffled by the beats of the music in her ears.

And . . . flip. And a jump, twist, land, performing a perfect cork—an aesthetically pleasing aerial trick that involved twisting on one's side in mid-air.

She raced to the playground and did a couple of bar laches on the monkey bars, walking on top of the bars and swinging back under every second bar or so, then swinging back up, the soles of her shoes against the bars. She hopped onto the rails from her perch on the long bar connecting all the shorter bars, and jumped from there to the middle of the slide, relaxing and sliding down to a halt near the bottom.

Her playlist switched to a slower, graceful beat.

She matched her moves to the music, swinging her legs over a low wall and over the rails separating the playgrounds from the concrete jungle. She made her way back to the wall she'd started her run with to catch her breath.

She ran up the wall, gripped the edge, muscled-up, and sat down.

And came face to face with a glowering Ethan standing with arms crossed on the other side.

"You frightened me," Leah barked a laugh, pressing a hand to her chest. His eyes flashed at her as he perused her sweating figure with angry yet appreciative eyes. Leah swallowed and tried to keep her hands from shaking with apprehension as she removed her earbuds and tucked them into her yoga pant's pockets.

Ethan hopped onto the wall beside her. Leah shifted away when he turned to her. She looked around. There were only a few inches between where she was sitting and the end of the wall. Her only choice was to jump down and run if things got out of hand.

When things got out of hand.

"It's time for us to finish our conversation." He stared at her, his mouth tight. "I do not understand why you have to go directly against me. Haven't I told you . . . ?"

"Ethan. I am not under your authority. My team has been working hard to make sure that everything and everyone was okay with this before we kicked off. I'm not trying . . . "

"Everyone but the guy who's trying to start up his own Parkour gym and group in the same area." Ethan kicked the wall below him, loosening a bit of mortar. "You think you can waltz in, take potential clients from under my nose, and get by? Offering low rates I could not even think about matching? With a maintenance-free environment you don't even need to pay a nickel for? With a team that works along with you? How old are you, even?!"

Leah stared at him, willing herself not to cower under this tirade. She opened her mouth, unsmiling.

"Are you through, Ethan?"

"It's your turn to prove you're doing something good for the *whole* community, Leah Jung." Ethan's voice was bitter. He clasped his hands, his eyes never leaving her face.

"Fine. Then listen up.

"We checked with the councilor. It is lawful to hold public lessons in this park, though we have to pay a certain fee for it every month."

"Nothing compared to the several thousand dollars . . . "

"I'm not finished, Ethan Simpson." Leah whipped her ponytail around as she turned to look him in the face. "We use this area in the summer. Then we're going to move indoors to teach the kids harder moves safely. As for the low rates we charge for the classes, that's because this is not a business for us. We—I and my team—are doing all this to make a difference in the lives of kids and teens in the area. We are not looking to steal other people's business—we are trying to reach lives by the saving power of God's love and strength, through enriching the lives of these people using this sport. As a traceur yourself, you know what it's like. This sport teaches one to overcome physical obstacles, which makes overcoming mental obstacles easier." Leah took a deep breath. "And yes, I am blessed to have a team that's stood by me and worked without complaint through hard times. It's been only four full months, but we've grown a lot closer together with each other and the teens. The money's not what's at stake here. What's at stake, what's really important, are the lives we touch through this sport. And one last thing. I'm twenty."

He took a deep breath, his eyes excited and demanding. "See? You still got your whole life ahead of you. Don't waste it on teaching a bunch of kids. Join my team. We'll be at the top of the world someday."

"I'm not interested in your plans, Ethan. I'm sorry." Leah shook her head. "Please, go, do your own business and leave me alone."

"If you'll do yours, I will stick to mine. But you can't blame me for trying when I see a girl flying around these walls by herself. You're really cute when you're all riled up." Leah crossed her arms in front of herself, beyond annoyed and not a little apprehensive about the look in Ethan's eyes. Or what he'd do to her. And to her team.

"I can't stop now, Ethan. The team has just begun to connect with the kids. Some of them are becoming more receptive to the Gospel. I'm really sorry if this impacts your business negatively, but . . . "

"As I said before, may the best team win." He turned to leave.

Leah's blood boiled, ringing in her ear. "Leave my team alone. It's not their fault. Don't touch the kids. Don't harm anyone."

He turned back to her, his stare cold, hard, and . . . something else that bordered on longing. Leah just stared back at him.

"So you admit you're doing this on purpose, and that it's all your fault. Very well. We'll see just how dedicated you are to this vision of yours."

CHAPTER SIXTEEN

Leah bowed her head in prayer as Pastor Michael ended yet another wonderful Bible study. Adding her own *Amen* to the closing of the prayer, Leah got up from her seat and took up her purse, preparing to leave.

"Leah, could you stay behind for a minute?" Pastor Michael glanced at Leah before shutting his Bible and dismissing the rest of the Bible study group. Men and women trickled out of the room, giving Pastor Michael his customary handshakes and thank yous.

Pastor Michael got up, rearranged the scattered notes in front of him, then sat across the table from her. "Javin has been telling me about your Parkour group. How is that going?"

Leah saw nothing but sincere interest and concern in her pastor's eyes. "It has been going great. There have been a few instances when we've had to discipline the kids, solve conflicts, and such. To be honest with you, it has been a huge growing experience. I've learned to trust God and my team, to rely less on my strength, grow in patience and long-suffering—"

"I can see how," her pastor commented with a laugh.

Leah smiled. "Exactly." She paused and frowned. How much of her struggles should she share with the man before her?

141

"Is there something on your heart, Leah?" Michael said, after a moment's silence.

Leah passed her left hand over her right. "Yes. I'm not sure how to say this, but . . . you see, a guy has been tailing our team for quite some time now. He's been trying to get us to stop, but I'm not giving up because of him."

"And yet . . . " Michael probed, laying his arms on the table and leaning forward, his eyes studying her face.

"Yet his words are getting under my skin. Things like—does this really work? Does this sport really help kids? Is it only for my own glory, my own enjoyment that I'm doing this? Is it pride?"

"He asked you all that?" Michael raised his eyebrows.

"Not exactly, but something he said led to thoughts like that." Leah forged on. "I'm starting to see some small fruit in what we've been doing. The kids have been more cooperative, the hardness and resentment against life have receded from their faces. But I'm afraid there's going to be no lasting difference. Once they learn this sport, that's all there is to it. Sure, they would learn how to move, be fit, have fun, and learn to overcome obstacles. But is there, *could* there, be anything beyond that?"

There. She got it out.

Silence. Leah took a few deep breaths, her eyes suddenly filling with tears.

"Sorry," she muttered, reaching for a tissue from the Kleenex box on the table. She dabbed at her eyes.

Pastor Michael crossed his arms, uncrossed them, then finally leaned back and sighed.

"Leah. What I'm about to say to you might not be something you'd like to hear. If you get through these doubts and solidify your vision in the Word of God, your faith in Him and the work He is doing through you would be strengthened. We all struggle with pride, but before I get into that, let me tell you a personal story about a kid I've helped in the past. Perhaps this will shed some light on your struggles, give you further motivation, and prepare you for what you might have to face. What I'm going to be reminding you of through this story will be a tough pill to swallow, but—bear with me.

"It was my first year being a youth pastor. I graduated to full service soon after, but during that one year, I learned more than any seminary school had ever taught me. Despite all the philosophizing, theorizing, and ideas, there was something missing, and God chose to show me what was missing through a dark and sorrowful experience." He paused to gather his thoughts, rubbing a hand over his chin. Leah shifted in her chair, eyes riveted on Pastor Michael.

"Kyle was a nice guy—seventeen, eighteen years old. A senior in high school, about to graduate with flying colors. I had a lot of hope for him. He was smart. He could answer any questions I threw at him. He was the Bible whiz of the students I was working with. He professed to be a Christian.

"Then everything crashed. Someone discovered he was taking drugs. He was increasing doses every other week. I'd asked him why, and he said that ever since his girlfriend dumped him, he'd been depressed. These drugs gave him a way out no religion ever could.

"I realized I was too involved in changing the outside of the person, helping them live their best life now, while neglecting to nurture and help their spiritual side. And it hurt to know I'd done wrong.

"Things for Kyle started to run downhill. His parents jumped on him, demanding to know why his grades were failing, and why he'd come home so late. He was detached from almost everyone who cared for him—his friends and family—and was depending on those who did not care to make sure he was walking on the higher ground—myself and the friends who gave him the drugs in the first place.

"I watched him struggle again and again. The temptation was too severe. He was hooked.

"I begged him to stop. Told him to seek help from his parents, friends, told him to take whatever drastic measure he must to get himself off, save what remained of his life, and turn back to God.

"I did everything I could in my human understanding to help the young man who was dying before my eyes. And wicked though it sounds, I was helping him out of desperation to save my job. Save myself, preserve my reputation.

"One night, he walked into my office. I'd been working later than usual and was just wrapping up for that day.

"I looked up with a smile. That smile faded when I saw Kyle.

"His eyes were sunken. His smile was gone. Pallor replaced healthy cheeks. His eyes were dead, accusing, looking at me.

"And in a voice that was not his, he told me nothing could help him now. He'd deceived everyone for so many years. Nothing could lift the burden off his heart. 'Not the Jesus you've been teaching me about,' he said.

"I was about to defend myself, but he held up his hand.

"He told me he knew what I was about to say. That God can save a person, forgive all his wrongs. But he believed that no God, however loving, could die for me. He just couldn't go on anymore. 'There's too much before me,' he said. 'Too many obstacles I have to face to be right with God and everyone else again. I can't take it anymore.'

"Tears ran down Kyle's cheeks then. He lifted a bony hand to brush them away. 'There are too many obstacles. Physically, mentally, spiritually. I can't overcome them.' He turned to go.

"The next time I saw him was at his funeral."

Pastor Michael bowed his head for a moment.

Leah stared at the pastor, her heart breaking for the young man who'd taken his own life.

"I have told only a handful of people this story. I felt that you had to hear it, know why I'm about to say this to you."

Leah nodded.

"I'm not speaking to only you, Leah, I'm speaking to all Christians, in all walks of life. Christ must be at the center of everything in life. He is your Savior—He must also be Lord. He must be the reason you do anything and everything. He is the center of everything you do, or else all is in vain.

"Now, here is the part where I must call on you to remember that I'm speaking from love and a desire to guide you back on the right and higher path.

"Parkour is not your identity. It is not what your group is about. It is not what you are teaching the kids. That is all second to living for God. Leading those kids to Christ. Showing them His love and power. Sure, teaching them to overcome mental and physical obstacles is all good, and something I wish Kyle was equipped to do, but beyond all that is the power of the cross and the Lord Jesus Christ. You must do all things through Him."

Leah nodded.

"Parkour is the platform you're using to expand and develop the kingdom of God. Focus on leading souls to Christ and keeping them on the narrow path. Your focus is not on just teaching them to overcome obstacles. You are to be light and salt to them, then to build them up, with your team, with this sport, but most importantly with God and His truth. Do you understand what I am saying, Leah?"

His voice was calm and gentle, his tone firm. Leah nodded. "I appreciate the confidence you have shown me by telling me that story, Pastor. I feel so sad for the young man that decided to take his own life."

"Don't let it happen to your kids."

"I promise, Pastor. And thank you for the encouragement—reproof, I should say. You are right in telling me these things. All the training, and different kids, and parents to look after tend to take away the main focus of why I'm doing this. I feel refreshed and ready to meet the world again—with God by my side." She smiled as she got up from her chair and collected her purse.

"You'll know you're doing the right thing when the devil cannot leave you alone. But you'll have to keep going—I know you can. Even if people start leaving your group because God and Jesus come up regularly in your speech and discussions. Even if anything happens to hinder you. Pray, ask the Lord for direction and guidance. And if the answer is yes, overcome that obstacle for God—and Him only. You, the kids, the team—all are secondary to the one Lord of your life. Make the Lord Jesus the Lord of your team."

"Thank you, sir." Leah reached over and shook his hand.

"May God bless you, Leah. Stand strong."

CHAPTER SEVENTEEN

"Owen, that was a much better performance. I'm glad to see that you've improved so much since a couple of weeks ago," Leah praised, smiling.

Owen shrugged, nonchalant. The emotions warring in his eyes—anger or sorrow, Leah could not decide which—did not let up. He shot her a glance out the corner of his eye.

"So what do I do now?"

Leah decided to leave the unspoken matter alone. She'll ask someone later. Something was wrong.

Leah checked her watch. "We still have twenty-five minutes to go. Why don't I show you how to do the crane? You could practice that against the wall."

Owen shrugged again and headed to the low walls a few steps to his left.

Owen got into position for a precision—knees bent, eyes on his goal—then jumped forward, landing one leg on the structure and letting his other leg hang downwards, toes leaning against the wall to support his hands, which held him up on the ledge.

His first attempt and he'd perfectly executed the jump. Either he was truly gifted, or he had a knack for copying other people's moves.

"Way to go, Owen! That was a solid crane," Leah called over, smiling.

Owen's smile seemed forced as he looked back at her.

Leah felt a tap on her shoulder. Someone sniffled behind her. She turned and faced Shana and Andrea.

Fat tears trickled out of Andrea's eyes. There were dark circles under her eyes, tear streaks down her cheek. "She suddenly broke down as we were training some bar work with the rest of the girls over there," Shana explained, letting go of Andrea's hand to wave at the monkey bars to their right. "She asked if she could talk with her brother about it." Leah nodded and called Owen over.

Owen paused, hopped off the wall, and walked over to his sister. "Andrea, stop bawling like a baby." His tone was gruff, yet vulnerable.

Andrea turned to Owen, her eyes refilling quicker than she could wipe them away. "It's not like you don't care. Grandpa died, too."

"Andrea . . ." Owen's voice cracked as he lowered himself onto the ground. He looked up at Leah. "Do you mind if my sister and I step back from training for a while? Both of our grandparents died yesterday."

"Take all the time you need. I'm so sorry." Leah squatted down on her heels beside the siblings and laid her hands on their shoulders.

Shana tapped Leah on her shoulder. "I'll see if I can take over for Guy." She lowered her voice. "He lost his father . . . maybe he could help them heal."

"Thank you so much, Shana," Leah whispered back.

The three of them sat and watched Shana leave.

Andrea sniffled. "We did not want to come today, but my mom had to go somewhere. I don't feel like doing anything today . . ."

"But just curl up into a ball and cry your eyes out." Owen finished for her. His tone was scornful, condemning, but it sounded like he agreed with her.

Guy arrived, his calm eyes taking in the situation. He nodded at Leah, and sat, making a circle with Leah and the twins.

"I know. I've felt that pain before. When my father died."

Leah prayed Guy's experience could somehow help these two teens grieve.

"Grandma and grandpa died together yesterday. Their car went out of control and slammed into a brick wall." Owen's voice was dead, sad beyond emotion. "The paramedics said the death was instantaneous, but they never know for certain."

Guy nodded, his eyes holding more emotion than she'd ever seen him express before. "My father was my best friend—at least for the last few weeks of his life. When I heard he was in a coma, I spent as much time as I could with him, hoping I would be there when he woke up." Guy paused, his eyes misting over. Leah reached and gave his hand a quick squeeze of support. She felt his hand stiffen, then squeeze hers back.

"He left so quickly after he woke up for a few minutes. I'm not even sure if he'd heard us say goodbye one last time. There are things I could have said, that I should have said, but never did." Guy looked away, his eyes gazing into the past.

"How do you bear that?" Owen's question was just audible.

Guy slowly turned his head back to the group, looking straight at Andrea. "I know I'll see him again one day in heaven. I'll tell him all those things I never got a chance to down here."

Leah took a deep breath. The silence that followed was punctuated by Andrea's sobs.

"How do you know for certain?" This from Andrea again.

Owen looked at Guy, then at Leah, and back at Guy for a minute before staring into space across the park, paying no attention to the other freerunning kids. "My grandpa and grandma had been telling us all about Jesus and grace, faith, heaven, and hell ever since we were babies. I never took it seriously."

"But it was true to Grandpa and Grandma. It's true to you guys, too. What is it all about?" Andrea questioned, her eyes filled with longing.

Guy and Leah looked at each other, silently praying for wisdom and guidance as they lead these children to the truth of the Word of God.

Leah shifted her position and looked the two children in the eyes.

"Christianity is about Christ. His word, His gospel, His love, and His righteousness. God created the world, but sin soon entered it through the first sinful act of mankind. Since then, the human race has never been holy and righteous again.

"The connection between us humans and God himself was broken by our sin. We are unholy and unrighteous. We deserve to die, to be sent into eternal damnation away from the presence of the infinite, Holy God." Leah paused. Owen nodded. He was following her so far. Andrea looked at the ground, tore at the grass, then refocused on Leah.

"But in His great love and mercy, God the Father sent His only begotten Son into this world to die for our sins. Jesus Christ was crucified on a cross and raised on the third day, thus becoming the mediator between us and God. He died in our place so that we could live with Him in heaven."

"If you repent of your sins and believe on the Lord Jesus Christ, in His death and resurrection, accepting this gift of eternal life, you have hope that one day you'll see your grandparents again in heaven." Guy finished for Leah. "Like I have hope that I'll see my dad again when I die."

"Mom used to read the Bible with us, talk to us about these things," Owen said quietly. "For some reason she stopped doing that a while ago." He shook his head to dispel unhappy thoughts and rose to his feet. "Guy, knowing that you've lost someone close to you helps. It's painful, but we'll get through it. But I'm not sure if I want to make the decision to get saved yet." Owen shrugged and went back to his training, some of the bottled-up sadness and anger gone from his face.

Leah turned to Andrea, who hugged her knees to herself and sighed. "My grandma had given me a Bible to read and study for myself. I've never understood why my grandma and grandpa would be so happy and joyful. Like my brother, I'm not ready yet, but talking to you and Mister Guy about that, and listening to his story helped a lot." She gulped and wiped away the last of her tears. "Please pray for us. My grandma used to pray with us . . . it's like a legacy that she's given us we're not ready to receive yet." She got up. "I feel better now. I'll get back to training with Shana." She walked away with a small smile.

"That's the first time I've spoken about his death like that," Guy said, more to himself than to Leah. "I'm glad I've been able to help them by sharing my own pain and faith."

"I'm sure they've been comforted more than I would have been able to no matter what I said because of the personal experience you have." Leah looked into his eyes.

"Every cloud has a silver lining. This seems to be the first I could see of dad's death. I hope they would find theirs soon." Guy pushed himself into a standing position and reached a hand to help Leah up.

She accepted the offered hand, pulled herself up, and smiled.

"We'll be praying for them. These kids need all the prayer we can give them. Now, let's get back to work."

CHAPTER EIGHTEEN

TWO WEEKS LATER . . .

Owen stepped up to the low brick wall, placed his hands on top, and then dropped into a cat-leap pose in preparation for a muscle-up training. Guy crouched in a similar position beside him on the wall, demonstrating the move, explaining in detail. Owen nodded.

"Now you give it a try. Don't let your feet touch the ground. Let one leg fall down beneath you, kick out and up against the wall, swing yourself toward the top, and then push with your arms to get your upper body above and over the wall."

"Got it." Owen looked at his hands, then grunted, doing his best to do as Guy had explained. In a couple of tries, he got over the wall.

Guy nodded in approval. "Do it twenty more times. Make sure it's in your head and muscles. I'll be back."

Owen opened his mouth to complain but was silenced by one stern look from Guy. Owen dipped his head moved back into position, then went through the muscle-up once more.

Guy turned to Leah. "This boy is doing great." He motioned at Owen. "That's . . ."

A scream punctuated the air, and Leah swiveled her head in the direction it came from.

A few yards away, Gina was on her hands and knees, wailing in pain. Paul was the first to reach her, with Vic and Jav coming up behind him.

"What's wrong, Gina?" Paul knelt beside her, taking her clenched hands into his own and brushing her braids from her face. Leah stepped closer and scanned the girl for injuries. Nothing too serious.

"I fell from the wall. My knee is all scraped along the calf, and I think I sprained my wrist." Gina sniffed. Tears carved rivulets down her dusty cheeks.

Paul wrapped his arms around the shaking girl, his large hands caressing her. He turned to Vic and Javin. "Could we get something to splint her wrist with? And some salve for her scrape?"

Leah could not help admiring the caring and authoritative role Paul took in this situation. She nodded. "Jav, could you get the first aid kit?" Jav bobbed his head once and sprinted away.

"I have to take care of the other kids." Vic pointed to Shana, who was doing her best to coach twelve kids at once. Guy was making his way towards them, but Vic waved him back, and the two best buddies continued on toward the group of teens.

"Here's the first aid kit." Javin tossed the waterproof bag onto the ground and zipped it open. He rifled through the packages, then handed a disinfectant wipe to Leah. "Here. You can help her clean her leg there."

Leah nodded, wiping at the red, skinned patch running down the side of the girl's leg. "You're blessed this injury is not too serious, Gina. It's only a shallow scrape."

"I know. I was doing the crane, then I slipped and tried to catch myself." She sniffed. Paul wrapped his arms tighter around her.

Leah observed this and exchanged a covert glance with Javin, who shrugged at her and turned to Paul. "Could you watch Gina for a while? I'll have to call her parents and tell them what happened." He looked at Gina. "You signed the waiver form?"

"I think so."

"Good stuff. I'll step away for a minute." He nodded at Leah. "You're free to go and get your kids back." He winked at her, then moved away.

"Are you okay, Gina?" Leah asked. The girl, her eyes dry and showing pain, nodded at her, then burrowed deeper into the crook of Paul's neck and shoulders.

Something seems wrong with this scene. Leah looked at Gina. She seemed to have gained weight over the past few months, around the mid-section.

She chalked it up to hormones and left it at that.

"I'll leave you guys here for a minute. I'll run over and check on a few other kids." She gave the two teens a nod, then headed in Shana's direction.

Shana ran towards her from a cluster of kids. She waved her arms at Leah. "Leah! Leah! Minnie needs help!"

Leah trotted over and reached the crying girl seated on the ground. She looked at Minnie. No blood. No broken bones. But the way she grabbed her shoulder and was biting back screams . . .

"Minnie. Look at me." Blue pools of pain turned to her. "Did you dislocate your shoulder?"

"I don't think so. It . . . It's still in the joint socket, but it hurts like crazy." Minnie's breath came and went in spasms.

"Probably just sprained." Shana crouched beside Minnie and wiped back the blond hair that had fallen across Minnie's cheeks for her. A small group of kids hung around, curious, and apprehensive. Shana looked at Leah. "She was doing her flips off the bar. A few perfect moves later, there was this one flip where she let go of the bar too late, causing her to overstrain the joint as she tried to regain balance hanging from one arm."

Leah shook her head. "What's wrong with you guys today?"

"This sport is what's wrong. This stupid park. Stupid moves. I'm so not going to do Parkour again." Leah knew Minnie spoke from pain and anger, but still, the despair and hurt in that voice nagged at her, triggering snapshots of that failed Kong-gainer, flashing them through her brain in slow motion. The months of pain and inactivity. Torture. She pushed through the bitter memories and focused on the suffering girl in front of her.

"Minnie. You're going to live through this." Leah focused on the girl before her.

"Do Parkour again, after it has given me so much pain?" Minnie threw back at Leah, her face twisted with disbelief and anger.

Dark, bitter memories threatened to surface again. She let the pain flow through her, then let them go. She had to be strong for the girl before her. Leah bent down to eye level, looking into the broken girl's eyes. "Don't let one injury get you down. Accidents happen. Recover, then get back into training."

"Overcoming obstacles, Minnie." Guy looked at Minnie, eyes contemplative. "That's the name of the game. That's what you have to do now. This is one more obstacle in your Parkour journey: let it refine your skills, sharpen your awareness, and hone your dedication." He paused.

Guilt stabbed Leah in the heart.

"That goes for all of us." He looked around the group, staring at each teen by turn. His eyes drilled into Leah's for one condemning second. She felt like a hypocrite, a counterfeit. Her actions did not match her words. Guy's voice broke through her thoughts. "Now, let's get back into training. Leah, I'll leave this girl in your care." He gave her a smile and walked away, half of the kids following him. Several other kids were walking away from Minnie and Leah, headed to where Shana was setting up pointers and markers for them to train jumps with.

Vic was nowhere to be seen.

Leah swiveled her head around, then locked a stare onto the two men in deep conversation with each other out by the curb. Vic. And someone else who looked too familiar.

"Minnie? Could you come along with me, please?" Leah held out a hand to the girl. "I need to see what that guy over there is doing here." Leah pointed at Ethan, who looked straight at her. Vic threw his hands around, his face tight, his voice raised with frustration.

"I'll sit with Gina. We'll lick our wounds together." Minnie's lips twitched into a smile; then she took a seat beside Gina on the ground.

"I'll be back in a minute." Leah strode toward Vic and Ethan.

"Stay out of this, please." Vic held out a hand to Ethan, his eyes pleading. "The kids need our help right now."

"Why are you here, Ethan?" Leah demanded, putting her hands on her hips.

Ethan turned his piercing blue eyes on her. "I'm trying to get your team member here to see reason. Your kids are going to leave you very soon if kids start getting hurt every now and then." He waved a hand at Gina and Minnie. He looked at Vic. "Tell her."

Vic looked at him, shaking his head. Ethan seethed at him, eyes blazing. "Do it."

Vic sighed. "He said he's starting a gym a few blocks away. He is looking for traceurs to work it out with. At Aerial 360." Vic grimaced. "He promises a bigger paycheck than Set Free has been able to offer."

"Vic. You're not leaving us. Money is nothing compared to the impact we are making on these kids." Leah covered her mouth with one hand. Kids dropping out of class—sure. Something like that would happen. But to have her own team turn their backs on her when she needed them most . . .

That was too much. She stepped right up to Ethan, digging a finger into his chest. "Stay. Away. From. My. Team."

Ethan grabbed her hand. Leah snatched it back, but Ethan was stronger and held on.

Vic stepped close behind her. "Let go of my girl." His voice was tight, possessive.

Ethan looked at her, his eyes narrowing. "Leah. I did not take you for a liar." His teeth ground together.

"Let me go." Leah gritted her teeth. Yanked on her hand. "I did not lie."

"This *boy* here said . . . "

"Leah, I'll never give up on . . . "

"What's going on here?" Javin's cheery tone was in stark contrast to their conversation. Ethan looked up in surprise.

His hands loosened. Leah twisted out of his grip and broke free.

"Hey . . . " He reached for her as Vic laid two hands on Leah's shoulders and spun her out of Ethan's reach.

Javin pulled on Ethan's shoulder, turning him to face himself. "You're Ethan Simpson! The guy that left Team Lightning." He grinned, slapping Ethan on the back.

"That's a more positive reception than your team members have given me," Ethan answered in a bitter voice. "Yes. I'm starting my own Parkour gym and group in downtown Toronto."

Javin's cheerful spirit did not let down. "That's great! We could train at your facility during winter."

"Fat chance, buddy. Your boss won't consider that option." Ethan glared at Leah, his mouth hard.

"You never mentioned it, Ethan. You only said I had to stop this. For your business." Leah jutted out her chin, crossing her arms.

"The gym has been finished for a while now. It is the business and the team itself that's lacking. And that's forcing me to take you down." He leaned closer to her. Vic's hands tightened on her shoulder.

"Ethan, why are you doing so much to stop us? Why can't we just work separately toward one goal?" Tears stung her eyes. She focused on keeping her voice steady.

Ethan let out an exasperated sigh, running his hands through his hair. His eyes softened, became vulnerable.

"Because the girl I fell for loved another. It's the only way I could get her to see reason, to join my side. Then she broke my heart, turned her back on my pleadings, continued to bring me down."

Leah could not find a word in reply.

Ethan looked at her in grim satisfaction. "You know who that girl is. Be careful. If you're not stopping, I'm not stopping either." He abruptly turned away and stomped down the sidewalk, hands fisted in his jeans pockets.

Vic gave her a side hug. "You've got some explaining to do, Leah." His voice was gentle, but the tone was serious—stern. As if she'd done something wrong. Because—she did.

"What was that all about?" Javin walked beside the two of them, forehead creased in confusion.

Leah slipped out from underneath Vic's arm, guilt, shame, and frustration bleeding into her voice. "Guys, I'm sorry for not telling you guys of our . . . competition earlier. But I'm not ready to talk about this yet."

Vic stepped up beside her, mouth open, ready to speak. Leah held up a hand. "I will. Soon. But not now."

CHAPTER NINETEEN

Leah clasped her hands together and looked around at the four faces staring back at her. She sighed. She'd been dreading this moment all through the training session Team Set Free and their teens had just completed at the Vault. Now, seated in the foyer of the gym building, nervousness had built up into a burden of shame and guilt weighing down on her shoulders. She stared through the windows at the downpour outside, unable to meet the eyes of her friends.

"I'm so sorry for not telling you all about Ethan sooner. I understand that I might have broken your trust this way. I hope you all could forgive me, but to repair the situation as much as possible, I will tell you as much as I know about this."

Vic nodded. Shana shifted in her chair, retying her ponytail. Javin, his eyes calm, clasped his knee and waited. Guy tilted his head.

She took a deep breath.

"I met Ethan eight months ago, back in April. I was training alone at the park, and he happened to be passing through. From that time on, I'd suspected that he had a . . . crush of sorts on me, but I'd brushed it aside as nothing serious. I had no idea it would grow to something obsessive." She cleared her throat, staring out the window at the Vault's parking lot. "He flirted with me, complimented me. I enjoyed it at first . . . maybe a little too much . . . but this was *Ethan Simpson*." Leah noticed Vic clenched and unclenched his hands. She pushed on. "Traceur extraordinaire. The one who had inspired me to take up Parkour in the first place.

"He warned me not to start my own group, but I still did. It was, and is still, God's calling for us. To help those in the community to grow, learn, and overcome obstacles. Be light and salt."

"He was the guy that showed up on our opening party, eh?" Javin raised an eyebrow, resting his elbows on his knees.

"Yes." She paused. "His threats started then."

"Threats. We had no idea we were under attack. You should have told us, should have warned . . . " Vic's eyes flashed at her.

"I'm sorry, Vic." Leah looked at him. "I thought I could keep this away from you guys and deal with it myself. I realize I've been wrong. We need each other."

Vic held up a hand. "Ahem. Guys, most of you don't know about this, but Ethan has offered to have me on his team. He promised more money and influence than Team Set Free could offer."

Shana bristled and glared at him. "And, of course, you told him there was no chance you'll be leaving us."

"I told him to leave my team alone," Leah said, looking at the floor. They should know everything. They had to.

"Apparently he's not good at receiving instructions. Now he's doing his best to tear this team apart." Javin rubbed his mustache, eyes conflicted.

"None of us are leaving. We're not giving up now. The kids need us. We're so close to helping them . . . "

Vic's words were cut short when the door swung open with a bang, and Gina stumbled in.

"Miss Leah! Team Set Free! I need your help right now! Paul is trying to . . . " Gina choked on her next words, wrapping her arms around her middle section—which was significantly more rounded than the first time Leah had taken notice of it two months ago.

The entire team rose to their feet.

"Gina, calm down." Vic stepped closer to her.

At the beginning of the class, Leah had wondered where Gina and Paul had gone, having received no message as to their where-abouts. But she assumed that their parents had some sudden change of plans, placed the incident out of her mind, and concentrated on the kids who'd come. Now . . . what was this?

Gina wailed, clutching her hands together. "I can't! I can't! He's going to . . . it was all my fault . . . the baby. . . he told me if I could not get anyone to help him." Her eyes were wide, begging, pleading. "I could only think of you guys. Both of our parents had dropped us off here earlier—before you guys even came. Then Paul and I left. Now . . . you guys have to come." Her voice shook.

"Where is he? And what are you talking about?" Javin gripped Gina's shoulders, trying to calm her down.

Leah looked at Gina again. Her round stomach was a *firm* round stomach.

"Paul is in his apartment, where he lives with his mom. He wants to take his own life because he got me pregnant." Gina stared at them all in turn, her wide-eyed gaze searing Leah with its desperate, hunted look. "He has given me a few minutes. There's no time to lose."

"We're all coming." Shana looked at Leah. "Leah. We're taking your car. Javin, you know where he lives. Drive us there."

The six of them sprinted to the Jeep in the parking lot. Shana leaped into the back seat, snatched Gina—whose adrenaline was draining out of her—and buckled them both in with Gina on Shana's lap. Vic and Guy squeezed into the two remaining seats, and Leah vaulted into the passenger seat beside a grim-faced Javin, who stepped on the gas once all doors were closed.

Shana muttered soothing words to Gina, her hands smoothing down the girl's thin arms. Gina's sobs filled the Jeep, tearing at Leah's trembling heart.

Pastor Michael's story ran through her mind as she recalled his warning.

"Don't let the same thing happen to your kids, Leah." She'd taken it seriously, but never thought it would really happen to them, to her.

Now she was racing to rescue a teenaged boy on the verge of suicide.

CHAPTER TWENTY

They arrived at the apartment complex. Javin flew out of the car, with Vic and Guy close behind. Leah made sure that Shana and Gina were okay before taking off after the three men.

The elevators would be too slow. She darted up the stairs, taking the steps three at a time, vaulting over the barristers whenever possible. She caught up with the guys on the third level.

Vic and Guy stared at Javin, mouths in a thin line. "What number?" Guy barked, his voice breaking with tension.

"201." Javin raced in the direction indicated by golden plaques on the wall in front of the stairs entrance.

Leah hesitated.

The elevator doors behind her opened. Shana and Gina stumbled out. Shana held Gina's shoulders, glancing at Leah with tear-filled eyes.

"A few months in. Her older sisters recommended an abortion. She decided to tell Paul first. She broke the news to him thirty minutes ago."

Leah nodded. She felt like reeling back from this heavy, discouraging, unexpected blow. But the team needed her. These two kids, broken and grieving, needed her.

Stand strong. Pastor Michael's voice sounded in her head. *May God be with you.*

"Come."

The three of them raced down the hallway and knocked on door 201.

Vic opened the door. His face was grim, with suppressed emotions. He gave Gina one undecipherable look and turned to Shana, nodding in approval.

"There's a couch in the living room."

"Were we too late?" Leah looked up at Vic, her heart thudding, expecting the worst.

"Thank God we came just in time." His eyes bore into hers for a second, a flurry of emotions. Then he reached a hand, touched her shoulder, and pulled her in. Leah looked around the small apartment, taking in the faded couches, rugs, wooden dining table, and flowered curtains.

"Where is he?"

"In the bathroom." Vic winced as the sounds of retching reached them from the washroom.

Leah moved to the dining table, her eyes drawn to the empty glass of water and two half-full pill bottles. She read the labels. Antidepressants, painkillers.

She was quiet. Vic laid a hand on her shoulder for a few moments, then left in the direction of the bathroom.

She'd never expected anything like this to happen. They were dealing with hurting kids. But not kids who were driven to the edge, looking for oblivion and salvation from the messed-up world in the depths of suicide.

"The devil won't leave you alone if you're doing it the right way." Pastor Michael's voice echoed in her mind. She cried out to God silently.

"Leah, could you get me a glass of water?" Shana spoke from one of the couches she was seated on. Gina curled up into a ball beside her.

"Sure." Leah walked over to the kitchen, switched on a light, and looked for a glass.

Her eyes lighted on a phone lying right side up on the counter beside the sink. A glass lay close by it. Leah crossed the kitchen, took the cup, and began to rinse the glass, filling it from the tap.

She glanced at the phone screen and saw a Google search for abortion clinics in their area.

Leah's heart sank. She took a deep breath, prayed for the two hurting teens in this apartment, and went out to the living room, handing the cup to Shana and sitting on Gina's other side.

"Here you go."

Gina held out shaking fingers, took a sip, then handed the glass back. Her eyes were unfocused, her body shaking with silent sobs. Shana tightened her arm around her shoulders.

"We're here for you and Paul, Gina. God is with us."

Shana reached out and gripped Leah's hand, giving and receiving support.

Vic and Javin came out of the hallway to their right, supporting a pale Paul between them. Guy brought up the rear.

The four of them sat on the sofa directly facing the three girls. No one said a word. Paul coughed twice, his eyes averted from everyone.

Finally, Paul looked up and cleared his throat.

"Team Set Free, thank you for coming to save my life. After Gina left to tell you guys, I decided to get it over with. I took three times the number of pills I should have, hoping that was enough to kill me.

"It almost did. But right where I'd almost died, there was nothing more I wanted than to live. I don't know—it's so hard to explain. I've wanted to die so badly, but at that moment, I wanted nothing else but to be alive, and stay alive." He paused, unsure of how to go on.

"I understand, Paul. I've been there."

Not only did Paul's face register shock as he turned to stare at Leah, but all her team members also turned surprised and pained expressions toward her. Leah nodded. Those memories were even darker and more bitter than the failed kong-gainer. "I've tried to take my own life before. It was one of the darkest, most hopeless parts of my life. But someone was praying hard for me. And just before I could do any to harm myself, I just could not. I had to live. I was filled with an absolute desire to be alive and to stay alive."

Paul nodded, relieved someone understood.

"Tell us what happened." Javin looked from Paul to Gina, his voice gentle.

Paul closed his eyes, taking a deep breath, then turned to Gina.

"Gina, would you mind if I tell them the whole truth? Even parts you know nothing about?"

This display of trust and thoughtfulness, even in such a tense and heartbreaking moment, brought tears to Leah's eyes.

Gina nodded, her eyes wide. "All three of us are safe for now. That's all I care about."

Paul nodded, then shifted his position on the sofa to look at the entire team.

"I guess I'll start from the beginning.

"Gina and I met a few years ago in middle school. Then we separated and went our different ways. You could say that I'd developed a crush on her, but she'd been too shy to notice me.

"Then I met her again at this Team Set Free. She was more beautiful than I remembered. I worked hard to impress her each training session. I praised her efforts each chance I got.

"She started to warm up to me, losing her shyness. I started to get bolder. Talking with her. Smiling, joking around. Touching her more." He paused, steepling his fingers. "One night, things got out of hand. We had sex. Short story—the condom broke. And I've made the girl I love pregnant at a time she's not prepared to be." He hid his face in his hands, unable to go on.

"I found out last week." Gina's soft voice broke the heavy silence. "My family pressured me for an abortion. But I knew it was wrong. So I decided to tell Paul first."

"I knew making love to her was wrong. And I still did it. But this baby growing inside of her is part of me. If I let her have an abortion . . . I know what a baby is, how it comes about. Does the life within Gina right now count as a human being? My teachers and friends tell me it's just a wad of tissue. Trust me . . . we all are. Just wads of tissue that walk, talk, and think with mental neurons synapsing with each other in our brains."

"Paul fought against the idea of my going for an abortion. But I have to unless someone supports me. I still have two years in high school."

"It's murder. Infanticide. What makes you and me more a human than the tiny living baby? I cannot have that happen. I could not live with the guilt knowing that I got an innocent girl pregnant, put her through the torture of an abortion, and forced her to live the rest of her life in regrets and what-ifs. One life—two lives destroyed because I did nothing. I'll kill myself before that happens."

"So he told me that if I was going to go to the abortion clinic, he'd kill himself." Gina wrung her hands.

"The shame and guilt are too big. Gina did not deserve this. The baby does not deserve this. It was all . . . "

"It's not entirely your fault, Paul. I was . . . "

"I should have stopped when we got too far. Instead, I just . . . "

"Stop. Paul. Listen. You've sinned. You and Gina have made a terrible mistake and acted in ways that anger God. But, so have we all." Guy spoke calmly, soothingly, yet with a tone of authority.

Vic laid a hand on Paul's rounded, hunched shoulders. "But there is hope. God sent His Son to take away our sin, covering us with His sinless, innocent blood so that we could be forgiven and stand righteous before God."

"If only you accept. Repent. Believe that He has died for your sins, redeemed your soul, set you free from the bondage of sin and the lies of the devil. And commit to living a new life that glorifies Him and seeks to honor Him." Shana patted Gina's trembling back.

Paul sat with his face in his hands. "You're saying that God sent His innocent Son into this mess of a world to die for me, and is willing to forgive all the wrong I've done in the past, forgive the hurt I've wrought on Gina, and change my life?"

"All that and more, Paul." Javin smiled as Paul looked up at him. "He promises to take you as His adopted child." He turned to Gina, who was listening, rapt attention, eyes intent on each of the speakers as they took turns sharing the gospel message. "But only by faith in Him."

Paul was silent. Thoughtful. "To repent means to know that I've done wrong, admit that I've done wrong, be sorry for what I've done wrong, ask for forgiveness from the one I've wronged, then do all in my power to undo the wrong and never to commit the same sins again."

"Exactly," Guy said. Leah nodded in agreement.

"Believing on the Lord Jesus Christ means that you truly believe that He is the Son of God, sent by God the Father, to come to this world and die for your sins," Javin explained. "That He allowed Himself to be tortured and nailed to a cross to bear your sins, to suffer what was your punishment. To die for the wrong that you've committed, Himself being innocent. Himself being God. Knowing that you are a worthless sinner."

"Jesus rose on the third day, once and forever overcoming the penalty of sin for us—death." Shana finished. "He is waiting with open arms, waiting for you to accept this gift of love, and fear Him as Lord. And Saviour."

Paul nodded, looking at Gina. "Are you ready? Do you want to do this with me?"

"It's a personal decision, Paul. It's between you and God, not a promise to someone else." Guy leaned forward on his elbows.

"I knew the gospel, but told him I was not ready to make the commitment to Christ yet. I wanted to live for a while." Gina's voice cracked with shame and regret. "I lured him away from what I knew was right." Tears dripped from her cheeks onto her clenched hands. "I see now the pain and sorrow sin causes. I can't bear living in hypocrisy and intentional sin anymore." It was Gina's turn to hide her face in the crook of her elbow. Paul shifted, as if he wanted to get up and comfort the girl, but Vic laid a detaining hand on his shoulder.

Shana placed her arms again around the girl, soothing her.

Leah looked at Paul. "What about you?" Her tone was kind, probing, yet firm. A challenge.

He looked at her, eyes filled with brokenness and repentance. "I'm done with feeling sorry for myself and for hating the guy who turned my life upside down. I'm done with living in sin and lust. If Jesus Christ would forgive me and receive me as his own, I will immediately and gladly receive his gift of eternal life and promise to live the life He has for me instead of listening to the devil."

Gina's face lit up, and she reached over to grasp Paul's outstretched hands, eyes brimming with joy.

"Hallelujah," Javin said as he turned in his seat and knelt beside the couch. With Paul and Gina kneeling in the center and Team Set Free surrounding them in prayer, the two teens dedicated their lives to God.

CHAPTER TWENTY-ONE

THREE WEEKS LATER . . .

"What's this I hear about kids getting battered up while doing Parkour?" The burly, red-faced man looked down his nose at Leah, who stood her ground against the aggressive stance of the annoyed parent in front of her. "I don't want my kid to end up with dislocated shoulders and skinned shins."

"I understand, sir, but small bruises and scrapes are part of the learning process. As the kids improve their skills, the risk of injury decreases."

"Risk? I signed up my kid to take risks on concrete pavement and brick walls?" The veins in his neck bulged. His angry voice resounded in the small foyer of the Vault.

Leah held up a calming hand. "I appreciate your concern, sir, but we progress reasonably. We do our best to make sure that the teens have all the necessary skills and confidence to take on a new move or variation of a move as they move forward."

The man uncrossed his arms. "I signed a waiver, so I cannot sue you for any injury my daughter would experience under your training." He made air quotation marks. "But I suppose I can withdraw my child from your team anytime I want?"

"Yes, sir. I could get you the forms to sign if you like."

"Here's the last payment for today's class." The man handed over two bills and stuffed his wallet back into his pocket with a scowl. "Where's the pen?"

Leah maneuvered to the other side of the Vault's front desk, picked a pen from the cabinet beside her, and handed it to him with a forced smile. She pushed a sheet of paper toward him.

"You are welcome to sign this agreement form."

He looked over the form. He picked up the paper and scribbled his signature on the bottom, wrote down the date and time, then shoved the sheet back at her.

"Let's get out of here, kid." He motioned to a fifteen-year-old girl Leah had worked with a few times in the past couple of weeks. Blonde, shy, and unassuming, the girl shuffled into her winter boots, gave Leah a small wave, and walked out of the foyer of the Vault behind her father.

"That's the third sign-off in the last two weeks," Javin commented, straightening a few things on the desk beside her. "Seems like things took a downward turn since the two girls got their injuries a month ago."

"The parents can't go without leaving us a well-wishing Christmas present a week before the holidays," Guy muttered, turning toward Javin and Leah from the doorway of the gym.

"Let's look on the bright side. At least the fourteen kids who signed up on the first month are still with us." Vic leaned against the desk, looking at his fellow team members with an encouraging smile before disappearing back into the small crowd of parents who'd congregated in the foyer, waiting to pick up their kids.

Someone waved at her. Leah recognized Ashlee's parents. She returned Vic's smile and made her way through the packed foyer to the two sober-looking Chinese parents.

"*Ni Hou*," Leah greeted with a smile—one that fell when the man and woman stared back at her without emotion.

The woman spoke first in broken English. "My daughter does not like the class. She said someone got hurt. We don't want her to come back." The father handed her the payment for today's class, his eyes averted.

A few heads turned in their direction; eyes narrowed at her.

"I apologize for what happened last week, Auntie. We will do our best to prevent such things from happening again."

"Thank you for the lessons she had. Maybe she would like to come back. But we do not want her to come anymore. It is too dangerous." The woman tightened her mouth into a straight line.

Leah took a deep breath and forced herself to smile.

"That is okay, Auntie and Uncle. We hope that we part good friends?"

"Maybe." The woman's tone said otherwise.

Vic came over, leading Ashlee by the hand. "Here is your smiling daughter." He gave the couple a smile, which the man barely returned.

Vic raised an eyebrow at Leah.

Ashlee stood as her mother helped her into her coat. She looked at Leah and Vic, eyes filling with tears.

"I'm sorry I have to leave, Miss Leah, Mr. Vic." Her English had improved somewhat. "My parents are very concerned." She groped for words but did not find them. Instead, she opened her arms and dove at Leah. "I will never forget you. And I will continue to jump, run, and play. Thank you for being a friend in a new country," she whispered into Leah's ear, her Mandarin slipping straight into Leah's heart.

Leah's eyes blurred. She nodded against Ashlee's shoulder.

"I'll miss you, too. I'll be praying for you." She gave her one more squeeze, then released her.

"Farewell." The man reached for his wife and daughter and left.

Leah waved at the retreating figures, wondering how many more students would leave them.

"Miss Leah? Paul and I would like to tell you and Team Set Free something." Gina materialized at her side.

"How are you doing, Gina? Paul?" Leah nodded to the subdued-looking young man hovering behind Gina, who was a head shorter than he was.

"Us three are doing great. We just wanted you guys to know that we've talked to both of our parents last week."

"You two are brave."

Gina smiled at Javin's praise. "Parkour training taught me to see it just as something I had to do, whether I wanted to or not. It was hard, but we did it."

"Together," Paul added, his eyes resting for one long second on Gina before turning to Vic and the rest of Team Set Free standing behind the front desk. "Our parents were hurt by our actions, but then we told them of our conversion to Christ, and of our decision to keep this child." Exclamations of joy came from each member of Team Set Free. Leah clapped her hands. Paul continued, "Our parents would help us take care of the baby and raise him up."

"Or her," Gina countered, smiling.

"Or her." Paul cleared his throat. "Gina is due in about four, five months. She's not exactly in shape to do Parkour."

"Understandably." Guy agreed, attempting to smooth over the embarrassment and making it worse.

Gina looked up at the five of them with flaming cheeks. "I won't be able to train for maybe half a year starting now because of the pregnancy, but I would like to come watch and see what I could learn."

"Our parents agreed that it's best that we take personal responsibility for what we've done—right or wrong, like what you guys have been showing us through Parkour."

Javin tilted his head, confused.

"Like, making our own decisions to push ourselves this day or wait until we have more energy. As this sport has taught us, a bad decision or bad calculation leads to bad results. And vice versa," Gina clarified.

Leah nodded, along with the rest of Team Set Free.

"Would you be okay if we pray over you both—and the baby—right now? Give thanks that your parents took this positively and that we're all safe and headed in a way that would glorify God, even if it started out wrong?" Javin held out his hands to the two young people now seated before them.

Paul looked at them with a grateful smile. "We'd appreciate it." Gina nodded, her face happy.

The team stepped forward, laid their hands on the teens, and prayed for them with full hearts.

The team tidied up the gym and prepared to leave.

Shana got up and headed over the coats rack. "We'll see y'all after the New Year. Vic's family and mine—and Guy's, too, probably—will be on vacation to for a couple of weeks. Family reunions."

"Sounds fun. I'll miss having you guys around. We'll get the scheduling and stuff back on track after the holidays."

"You all just want to leave us two here to brave the cold." Javin mock-complained, leaning against the wall closest to where Shana was arranging her scarf around her head.

"We'll miss you guys, too." Shana looked at Javin, her eyes shining. Then she reached over and gave Javin a hug. It caught him by surprise, but his answering smile was wide.

He gave her a squeeze and released her. "Be strong. Be happy. Be you. Everywhere, anywhere."

"God bless you, brother. And Leah." Shana nodded at the two of them before turning to the door Guy held open. Guy lifted one hand in a farewell salute, and the door closed behind them.

Vic lingered behind, taking his time putting on his coat and gloves. Javin watched him. Leah straightened the scattered chairs, feeling somewhat sad knowing that Vic would be leaving Toronto—her—for the next few weeks.

Suddenly he stood before her, a wrapped box out-stretched toward her. "Here. Take it. Merry Christmas."

Leah looked up, curious. Their hands brushed as Leah reached for the medium-sized box.

They stood holding the box together, their eyes locked in a long, silent stare.

Javin cleared his throat—loudly, against the otherwise silent foyer. Leah looked away first. "Thanks, Vic. I appreciate it. I'm sure I'll love . . . whatever is inside." She paused and looked back up at him. His eyes were filled with a vortex of emotions. His eyes demanded hers, intense. She looked back at him, confused.

A car's horn blared from the entrance. Leah and Vic turned to see Guy's wave and Shana's teasing smile.

Vic held up a detaining hand at the two impatient people and gripped Leah's hand. "I'll be back."

"I'll be waiting, Vic." She heard Javin smother a laugh behind her. Leah shrugged at him. What she said was the truth.

"I'll see you when I come back. God bless you till then." He released her fingers and turned, reaching for the door handle. Then he was gone.

Leah turned the package around in her hands.

Javin walked up beside her. "You won't see what's inside if you keep doing that." He tossed her a smirk.

She looked at him. "What are you still doing in here, Jav? Don't you have somewhere to go? It's getting late." Leah lifted an eyebrow at him, smiling.

"I could say the same to you." He joked back. Then his face grew more serious, and he ran his hand over his mustache. "What's going on between you and Vic, if I may be so bold?"

Leah tilted her head, narrowing her eyes. "Nothing at all. Why do you ask?"

"Y'all could have fooled me." Javin raised an eyebrow at her. "I just have your best at heart. From the way Vic looks at you and the way he always looks out for you . . . " He paused. "Slight change of subject, but . . . "

Leah smiled at his hesitation. "You want to ask me something about Shana?"

He flushed. "Was I that obvious?"

Leah laughed out loud. "Do I have to repeat everything you just said to me about Vic to your face?"

"Shucks. I thought I was playing it cool."

"Didn't you two hit it off at the start? Sparks flew on the first day, if memory serves me right."

"You do have an impeccable memory. And I want to let you know that your bossing skills have improved." Javin winked and put on his jacket and beanie.

He paused. "Be strong."

"Be happy." Leah looked into his eyes, finding in them the strength they'd always held.

"Be you," they said together. He waved and left.

CHAPTER TWENTY-TWO

Shana shook off the raindrops on her jacket's hood, stepped out of her boots, and slipped into a pair of well-worn running shoes.

"Here. Let me help you hang that up." Javin got up from his seat in the Vault's foyer and reached for the damp jacket.

"I got it. But thanks for offering." Shana flashed Javin a smile and hung it on one of the empty hooks near the entrance.

Leah sat at the front desk, watching the interplay between two of her dear friends with a wistful smile. Chemistry was at play here.

Javin lowered himself onto the chair he'd risen from. He looked at the clock on the wall behind Leah.

"Vic did not get the memo about the indoor class we were doing today?"

"Because of this thunderstorm that decided to come by to match our changed schedule?" Shana added with a wry smile.

Leah checked her email on the computer in front of her. Nothing new. "I believe he is trying to hand in tests he took for the end of the semester. He told me he might be running late." Leah frowned at the storm outside. "From the look of things, he might not be able to go in at all."

"Guy's already here, is he?" Shana asked, looking from Javin to Leah.

"Yes. Some of the kids are here already." She paused. She could hear laughter and running feet. "Sounds like they are having a blast in there." Shana stared at Javin. "You came before me. That sounds like a handful for Guy to manage on his own. Why are you not helping him out?"

"I had to give you a proper welcome and escort you into the inner court of indoor Parkour." Javin smiled at her, rising again. Shana's cheeks warmed.

Leah smiled to herself as Javin opened the gym door with a flourish to let Shana in, then frowned as he allowed the door to close behind himself without a glance at Leah following them right behind him. "Watch it, bro." She caught the swinging door just before it slammed into her face.

Shana made her way to Guy, throwing Leah a smirk, who returned it with raised eyebrows.

Javin stepped to the teens gathered around where Guy was demonstrating a double kong-gainer over a training obstacle. Watching him perform the move sent shivers down Leah's spine. Fear coursed through her. She shook off the numbness. Javin called out. "Impressive, Guy. Now boys and girls, let's get to work." He clapped his hands together three times, smiling as he saw reluctant faces turn toward him. "I know that move looks cool, but you've got to be able to do a lot of other ones before you could do something like that."

"Let's get moving." Guy bowed to the dispersing group and straightened with a smile. He glanced at Leah, eyes probing. She gave him a weak smile—all she could muster—hoping he did not see the fear that must be all over her face. She shrugged and turned away from those intelligent, unrelenting eyes.

Leah did a quick headcount and came up with eleven. Gina was missing.

She looked at Shana, a question in her eyes.

"Gina's over there." Shana motioned toward a chair near the left farthest corner of the gym. "She'd like to rest awhile, maybe opt out of the more active moves. She told me she could do precisions when we get around to it."

"Thanks, Shana." Leah smiled at her friend, waved at Gina—who waved back with a small smile—then took three of the four boys and moved toward the foam pit. The foam pit was surrounded on two sides with foam mats, with a rectangular hole in the ground filled with pieces of foam. The impact of landing—especially for aerial tricks—would be minimized in the foam pit.

Leah greeted the boys by name, then began to demonstrate and explain the new move they were going to learn.

"Take a couple running steps, block and jump, then flip your upper body over, swing your arms down, and tuck your knees in. The tighter you tuck in your knees to your chest, the faster you'll rotate."

Leah did so, landing in the foam pit feet first. She climbed out and motioned to the first boy. "Make a line, shortest to tallest. You all have done the backflip before. This is basically the complete opposite of a backflip—you're going to propel yourself through the air with your upper body, instead of your knees. And of course, you're flipping forward, not backward." Leah waved the first boy on.

Leah watched the boys do their flips, made sure they had correct form and momentum, told them to keep practicing in turns, then turned to where Andrea and Minnie were practicing lines using the gym's bar structures, pseudo-brick walls, and wooden obstacles. She made sure Shana was keeping an eye on them before making her way to where Gina sat, watching the kids' movements and interactions with longing and interest.

"Hey." Leah smiled at the girl. "You ready to train a few precisions?"

The girl shrugged, laying a hand on her stomach. "I guess I could try." Gina got up with a tired smile and walked over to a couple of precision trainers lying five feet apart and stepped one leg up.

"I think that's a good distance to work on and keep yourself in shape. Don't push yourself, though. If anything feels hard . . . "

"What's wrong with that chick? She got a disease or something?" One of the rougher boys pointed at Gina's midsection, a sneer on his face. "Or maybe she's been having . . . "

A form whizzed past Leah's side and slammed full force into the bully, knocking him to the ground. *Paul.* Leah spun to her left to see where he'd come from and looked up at a shocked Javin, standing on top of the pseudo-brick wall.

The two boys were rolling around on the floor, wrestling with each other. The bully who'd insulted Gina had to be significantly bulkier, taller, and heavier than Paul, but he was clearly no match for Paul's lean, flying limbs. Paul's face was alight with fury as he pounded the guy below him. The boy held onto Paul's flailing hands, using his brute strength to keep Paul's fists from his face.

Several other boys hopped onto them, trying to tear the two apart. Fists flew. Angry words were exchanged.

Then the girls got into the action, throwing bits of foam around at the boys, at each other. Names were called. The voices grew louder, angrier. Every single teen, with the exception of Gina, was engaged in an all-out brawl. Leah was stunned, shocked beyond words.

In a daze, Leah looked around, not being able to comprehend how everything could crumble like this in mere seconds. All the hard work she and her team had placed into molding and building these kids up—gone. They've lived through ten months together, sharing triumphs, sharing pain.

A piece of foam landed at her feet. Her eyes went to it.

Crooked edges, like the stones on top of the brick wall she'd almost vaulted over years ago. A broken piece of garbage. Useless on its own. Yet, when gathered together with hundreds of similar pieces, they created the safest training platform available on which to learn and improve amazing skills.

She felt like that piece of brokenness right now.

Yet her team must stand strong, stand together. The kids must put down their hurts and their differences, forgive each other, and rebuild the trust and relationships that had just been broken.

Leah lifted her head and scanned the chaos of enraged, excited kids. Her eyes fell on Gina, who stood in the center of it all, hugging her arms around herself, her posture one of utter despair, sorrow, loneliness, and confusion.

Leah walked over to Gina, who looked up with tears in her eyes when Leah tapped her shoulder. Leah gave Gina a reassuring grin. "I'm sorry, Gina."

"It's all my fault. I should not have come. If I hadn't, that boy would not have said what he did." Gina placed her head in the crook of Leah's shoulder and burst into tears.

Someone bumped into her. Shana. She was in tears. A red welt was beginning to form on the side of her face.

The gym was a mess. She was a mess. Everything was a mess.

Leah's phone beeped. She reached into her pocket to find a new text message.

Come to the arbor in the park immediately. I need your help right now. Something is very wrong. Vic.

He must have had an accident. In the shock and confusion of the moment, she forgot to check the caller ID. She gripped the phone in her hand, trying to understand what was happening.

She looked at Guy, who was doing his best to hold down a couple of boys trying to hit the boys under Javin's arms a few feet away. She saw Owen in the mess, but she could have been mistaken.

She looked around. Foam bits from the foam pit were everywhere. Shana gripped the hands of three sobbing girls as she, tears running down her own face, was trying to explain what had just happened. "Leah: we need you. The kids are out of control."

She turned to Shana, eyes desperate. "Shana. Something is wrong with Vic. I must go right now. I . . . God be with you all. You can do this."

Leah sprinted out of the gym, flew past the foyer, and out of the building, snatching her raincoat at the last minute. She vaulted into her Jeep and spun out of the parking lot, heart thumping.

CHAPTER TWENTY-THREE

THE PARK CAME INTO VIEW.

Leah flew out of her jeep the second her car stopped moving. Sheets of rain immediately drenched her. Lightning and thunder flashed and crashed in the distance. She stood for a few dazed seconds on the curb, eyes darting around for signs of an accident, an emergency.

There was none.

Heart in her throat, Leah sprinted to the wooden arbor, guided by the spike sitting atop its six-sided cone-shaped roof. The arbor was deep in the center of the park, almost all the way next to the other street. She reached it, bounced up the couple of concrete steps, and stood in the center, eyes scanning the six wooden beams and five waist-high walls surrounding the arbor.

It was empty. Stark empty.

"Vic? Victor!" Nothing but the torrents of rain answered her call. She darted around the arbor, looking under the seat in the center, peering over the walls at the grounds below, even looking up into the beams that crisscrossed themselves inside the roof.

No one. She searched the grounds beyond the last wall with her eyes, her back toward the entrance of the arbor. What could have happened? Why would Vic have called her here?

"Wonderful weather."

Leah spun to face the speaker, heart thumping. Ethan stood a few feet away, hands in his pockets. A flash of lightning silhouetted him against the bleakness of the rest of the park, revealing his tense shoulders and resolute stance.

Leah stared at him as conflicting emotions warred within her. She kept her mouth closed.

"I didn't think you would come." He stepped closer, brushing raindrops off his rain jacket. She felt, instead of saw, his eyes travel over her soaked clothes and drenched hair. She looked at him for one more second, then immediately turned away. Her eyes instinctively sought a way to escape. The normal exit was directly behind Ethan— and beyond that was her car. Her other option would be to get over one of these walls.

Then she remembered what was happening at the Vault and made her decision.

She placed her hands on the horizontal plank behind her and hoisted herself up and over.

Except—the "over" part never came.

A hand gripped her shoulders and yanked her back to the ground. The slick, damp wood slid from her fingers. Her feet touched the ground.

"You're not leaving yet." Ethan reached for her other shoulder, but she ducked away from both of his hands and turned to face him.

"I am. My team needs me right now, more than ever." Shana's desperate tears and Guy's despair flashed across her mind. She darted a glance around the arbor. There was just enough space between Ethan's left side and the arbor. If she could squeeze past him in a sprint and get out of the arbor before he could give chase . . .

She moved. Leah kept her head down, eyes glued onto the exit. She picked up her speed.

And slammed straight into the arm Ethan held out to stop her. He spun her around and held onto her with both arms. "Yeah, I know what's happening to your team and your kids at the Vault. That's why I must keep you here until everything blows up beyond repair."

Fury, despair, and determination coursed through her. She glared at his smug face and brought her elbow up, driving it into the side of Ethan's neck. His grip on her waist loosened; she took a step back and paused to take a breath to try and calm herself down.

Ethan closed in, his eyes flashing against the shadows cast by the occasional lightning. Before he could touch her, Leah gave him three rapid-fire rib kicks, her leg snapping upwards at an angle and making contact with his ribcage. She could not tell if he winced or not, but he squeezed his eyes shut for just one second.

That was all she needed. She shifted her stance and gathered momentum, sending her right foot toward his head in a roundhouse kick. Ethan stumbled backward.

This was her chance. She placed her hands on the wall behind her and jumped, almost clearing it.

Something snagged at her foot and wrapped itself around it. Ethan yanked her back in. "You're staying here until I let you go."

"No, I'm not." She shot back. Then she yanked herself forward, arms pumping, heading straight toward the exit.

Ethan stuck his foot in her way. She jumped over it but slipped on the wet concrete. She brought both of her elbows up to shield her face from the impact and braced herself for the fall.

The concrete rose to meet her, and she rolled to minimize the impact. Tiny pebbles dug into her skin, but she had bigger problems to deal with than physical pain.

Ethan had her pinned to the ground before she could recover from her fall. His voice was tight, his eyes looking down into hers, his knee on her hips. "Now, would you listen to me?"

She didn't answer. She didn't struggle, either. She would conserve her strength and fight her way back onto her feet when the timing was right.

Ethan's voice grew thoughtful. "I'm jealous of everything you have, Leah Jung. Everything you do. Everything you love." He paused. Leah tried not to listen, tried not to let herself feel any sympathy for the man who would deceive her and detain her like this in order to ruin Team Set Free. "No one knows who I was before I joined Team Lightning. No one knew how I fought just to survive, how I had no one to care for me when I was young, how lost and scared I felt then and still feel now."

"Why are you telling me now? Because I'm helpless?" Leah shifted under his knee, moving her legs beneath her and planning her next move. But the pain in Ethan's eyes made her pause and regret her sharp words.

"Maybe. You broke my heart, and I've been trying to separate you from everything you've loved or cared about ever since. So you could know just how you've crushed me. Call it revenge if you will."

Leah absorbed the information. "So it's not just business." She tried to distract him from his grip on her supine body. "I never knew it was this personal."

Ethan leaned his face closer to hers. "Very personal." He leaned in even closer, shifting his knees to maintain his balance.

That was her chance.

Leah wrenched her arms from his grip, administered an elbow to his sternum, rolled from underneath him, and was on her feet before Ethan could recover. Unwilling though she was, she had to get him down if she was going to go back to her team any time soon.

"Leave me alone, Ethan. It's not going to go nicely for either of us if you don't." She faced him squarely.

He lifted his head. His hands fisted. His eyes hardened.

She had no choice. She'd wasted too much time already. She took a deep breath and flew into action.

Before he could rise from his knees, she grabbed his head, forced it down, and brought her knee to his face thrice in quick, forceful succession. Then she shoved him backward with her hands, adding a well-aimed kick to his chest. His head flipped back, his legs bent, and his body fell onto the ground.

Leah didn't even glance at him before turning around and vaulting over the side of the arbor. She landed in a puddle of murky water, but couldn't care less. She had one goal—to make it back to the Vault as soon as possible.

She couldn't believe she didn't even think to make sure that the text came from Vic. If only she'd taken a minute to verify with Shana, all this—the fight, the time lost, the pain from her scraped elbows and the bruises on her knees and shins—did not have to be. But now it was too late. She'd made her mistake. Now she had to deal with it.

She picked up her speed and sprinted past the trees, bushes, and picnic tables that dotted this side of the park. Water splashed onto her from above and below. The gray clouds, the thunder, and lightning all came together to create a rather epic, eerie impression.

She ran. The hedge of bush and trees that lined the border of this side of the park partially hid what she was looking for—a wrought-iron gate that opened into the street beyond.

Several problems greeted her as she approached the gate. One—it was much higher than she'd anticipated, reaching up to her chest. Two—the gate was padlocked tight. And three—rapid footsteps sounded behind her.

She'd forgotten that Ethan was a professional athlete.

CHAPTER TWENTY-FOUR

SHE KEPT SCANNING HER SURROUNDINGS for any other exit. The spaces between the iron bars were too narrow for her to squeeze through. The rain made the gate too slippery for her to climb over the gate. There had to be another way out. There—a tree branch reached across the path just in front of the gate. If she could only jump that high . . .

She had nothing to lose. She launched herself into the air, grabbed the branch, and held on—barely. She swung herself forward twice to build momentum. Each swing on the rain-slicked branch caused her hands to slip a little, and her grip weakened. On the third swing forward, she lifted her knees to her chest and threw herself forward. As her hands left the branch, she straightened her legs and arched her body over the gate.

Leah landed on the balls of her feet, bent down, touched the concrete with her hands to absorb part of the shock, then broke into a sprint down the sidewalk.

Ethan landed in a similar fashion just behind her—at least, that was what she assumed. She did not look back. Somewhere before her, a small street or alley to her right would lead her back to the street the Vault was on.

She kept running, but she could not move fast enough. Her clothes clung to her body. Puddles of treacherous water were every-where. And then there were the big cracks in the concrete . . .

She caught her foot in one of them and fell forward. Instinctively, she rolled forward and was back on her feet in an instant. Ethan was close behind now. Too close.

She turned into a narrow alley on her right between two brick buildings. Garbage and garbage cans littered the ground, leaving only a narrow path down the middle. Rusty metal stairs zigzagged up the sides of the buildings. The windows and doors were all closed against the rain and thunder. She paused for one millisecond, unsure. An idea came to her; she turned to her right and ran deeper into the shadows.

A bolt of lightning flashed directly above the alleyway. A large garbage can was in front of her. It stood between her and the flight of stairs before her. Swallowing her disgust, she raced at it, speed-vaulted over the obstacle, caught one of the stair steps from below with her hands, and pulled herself through the gap between the steps.

Thunder boomed, and she almost missed hearing the footsteps turning into the alley behind her. Leah clambered up to the nearest landing and huddled in the darkest corner, away from where Ethan would see her if he looked up from the alleyway.

She peered at him from her crouched position. He had stopped and was looking around for her. Then his eyes fixed on the garbage bin she had just vaulted over. He made his way to it.

Leah held her breath and moved just enough for her to see what it was he was staring so intently at.

She'd left a handprint. She'd used her hand to brace herself as she cleared the bin in a vault.

His eyes traveled up toward where she was hiding. She could do nothing to trick him now—with his experienced eyes, he immediately saw what route she would have taken after the vault.

She saw him gather himself for a jump toward the stairs. He'd already seen her.

She ran up the next flight of stairs, reached the landing, and gauged the distance between the rail she gripped in her hands and those of the landing directly across from her from the flight of stairs beside the one she was on. She could barely make that distance on a good day. But in the rain?

She'd trained in all sorts of weather. The philosophy behind parkour was to be ready to act, to move in any and all situations at any time. But this was for real. She looked down at the ground below her. If she missed, it wouldn't be fun.

Then, the stairs shook as Ethan bounded up the steps below her.

She clenched her teeth, pulling herself onto the rail until the soles of her feet balanced on top. A cat leap should do it: a precision jump from this rail to the other under such circumstances was simply too risky. She breathed a quick prayer, forced all fear out of her mind, and focused completely on the moment.

Her arms swung forward. Her legs pushed off. Her feet left the comparative safety of the rails. Her eyes fixed on the spot she would land on. Her body adjusted to the landing in mid-air. Her feet touched the rails, absorbed most of the shock; her hands followed, gripping the top of the rails; then her legs folded under her, and she hung off the rails outside of the landing.

She shot a glance behind her. Ethan was right behind, about to execute the same move. She had no time to vault over the rail and run down the stair like she'd planned.

She looked down. It would be a big drop were she to fall or jump onto the landing below her, but she had no choice.

She unfolded her legs and let them hang. Hand over hand, she lowered herself using the horizontal bars of the railing until her hands gripped the metal floor of the landing.

She looked down again. And let go.

She fell onto the hard metal floor, rolled to absorb impact, then got back to her feet and pulled herself into a vault over the rail and onto the pavement below. Ethan was right behind her, but she had no time to care.

She darted out of the alley, checked the street signs with a single glance, and then broke into a run toward the Vault. The thunder and lightning had passed over them, but the rain had not lessened. She could feel the water droplets washing off the dust and grime she'd accumulated in the alley.

A few pedestrians trotted up and down the sidewalk, eyes lowered and hands gripping umbrellas. She wove her way through them. Benches, concrete waste collectors, and oversized flower planters were scattered across her path. She bounded from one structure to another if they were close enough, vaulted over some, and ran around the others.

She strained to hear Ethan's heavy breathing and footsteps behind her, but there were none. Some of the adrenaline which she'd been feeding off of drained out of her. The chaos at the Vault when she'd left resurfaced in her mind. Guilt, despair, and bitterness drove her on.

She blinked away the water in her eyes and charged toward the low wall before her that separated some of the buildings from the others. Her mind was focused not on what was before her or even what she was about to do, but with what had happened with her friends and those she was teaching, and what she could do to build them back up once she got back to them.

Her hands reached toward the wall and pulled her body up and over, with her bent legs passing through her arms. A small smile spread itself on her face. She'd forgotten how fun kong vaults were.

Something in her subconscious mind clicked. Without thinking, she threw herself backward into a gainer right after she cleared the wall.

She landed on her feet and continued running, her mind barely registering her own movements as she continued to sprint toward the Vault. The concrete slabs in front of her looked familiar. It wasn't until she'd performed precision jumps from one of them to another that she recognized them as the ones she'd trained from the first time she'd laid eyes on Ethan.

She looked over her shoulders and saw him sprinting towards her. She had no time to lose. She made her way past the flowerpots. The entrance to the Vault was finally in sight. She slowed down just enough for her to grab the door handle and yank the door open.

There were no sounds of fighting from inside the vault at the moment. She held the door open for one moment, turning her head to look through the glass at Ethan.

He leapt onto one of the concrete slabs she'd just passed—the exact one she'd been standing on the day he came into her life, if she remembered correctly. He stood there in the rain, streaks of dirt on his drenched clothes, his blond hair plastered on his head, the intensity of his stare burning through the glass and space between them.

Time seemed to stand still. She met his glare confidently, silently, and even a little sadly.

Then the fight left his body. His shoulders sagged. He stepped down. He stared into her eyes for a few seconds more, then turned his back to her and walked away.

CHAPTER TWENTY-FIVE

SHE STUMBLED INTO THE FOYER, the door closing behind her. Exhaustion and pain overwhelmed her, and she fell into the nearest chair. Her clothes were soaked: within a minute, she was shaking from the cold and the letdown after her adrenaline had disappeared. Her elbows and hands were bloodied where metal and concrete had cut into them. Her shoes were scuffed, her hair a mess.

But at the moment, she was safe.

Leah let her head fall forward, catching her breath and allowing her racing heart to calm down.

Then she remembered the kong-gainer she'd executed minutes ago. It had been effortless. Her eyes opened with the realization. She'd been so focused on getting back to the Vault—here—as quickly as possible that she hadn't even realized she had just overcome her largest fear. Now that obstacle was past . . .

And she felt nothing but great heaviness. She felt weak. Helpless. Tired. Even her personal victory did little to relieve the sorrow in her heart. Her teens were hurting, and she couldn't help them. She just couldn't. Everything she'd worked for was coming apart. And there was nothing she could do to undo what was done.

No one but God Himself, nothing but the power of the Holy Spirit and the Word of God, could fully and completely heal broken, tired, and sinful human beings—including herself.

Still trembling in her soaked clothes, she rose and dropped to her knees, leaning her elbows on the chair. Tears came unbidden. "Father God." She choked on the words, aware of how undeserving she was of His mercy. "Show me what do to. I'm so tired. So afraid to make mistakes. I don't want to lean on my own strength or convictions or abilities anymore. I can't do anything." She wiped away tears with a damp hand. "I don't know how to face what's ahead of me. I don't want to fail. I can't let those girls and boys down." She cried out in the empty room, gripping her hands together, squeezing her eyes shut. "Lord, tell me what to do. I'm so weak and helpless. Our team can do nothing of eternal value without Your strength and grace, Lord. Help us. Help us Lord."

She remained on her knees, lost in wordless thoughts and fears, fighting back doubts with memorized passages of Scripture. Slowly, her heart and mind calmed, and her sobs lessened.

Someone opened the door and stepped in. Then a coat was draped around her shoulders, and a hand gently began brushing away the hair on her face.

She opened her eyes. Vic was kneeling beside her, searching her face with intense, concerned eyes. He looked into her eyes. "What's wrong, Leah?"

His quiet, kind voice threatened to bring back all the tears she'd just managed to staunch. She looked away. "I . . . I'm just tired and confused. I'll be okay in a bit." She smiled a little and pushed herself to her feet.

Vic took her hands and flipped them over. Leah pulled them away. She needed to be with the teens now. She didn't need to be fussed over. Vic held onto them, then looked at her elbows. He looked down at her shoes, then turned his eyes back to her face. His voice became strong, stern. "Leah. Tell me what happened." Before she could open her mouth, he stood up and zipped up his coat on her.

"You're freezing. Don't tell me I don't need to take care of you right now. I could get some towels or a new set of clothes for you if you have any." He paused when Leah shook her head.

"I didn't bring any with me, Vic. And we have more important things to do right now. The kids . . . " Leah's eyes filled again. Why was she so vulnerable when she had to be strong for her team and the teens? She swallowed and forced the sobs back down, along with her exhaustion and frustration. "The kids began fighting with each other a while ago. All . . . everything broke loose. I don't know what happened afterward, or is going to happen now." She turned and wiped the tears away. Then she faced him again, standing tall, meeting his eyes with a quivering smile.

Vic was silent. Then he reached out his arms and held her. "I don't know what you've just been through, Leah. I wish I'd been there for you." He stepped back, laid a hand on her shoulder, and tilted her chin to look into her eyes. "We're going to talk about that later. But you're right. Let's ask the Lord for wisdom and strength, and then we'll face whatever greets us inside those doors together." He held out his hand, and she placed hers into his, and he led them into prayer for the work ahead.

"Dear Lord, we come before You, beseeching You to fill us with Your spirit and power as we serve and lead the teens that have been training under our team for the past ten months. We pray that Your will be done in all that we say and do the next few minutes, and in the days that follow. I do not know what has happened here, but Lord, You know. May you give us the strength and courage to do the right thing by these teens, and heal all that has been broken by conflict that occurred earlier today. We pray all this in Jesus' name, Amen."

"Amen," Leah added. She opened her eyes, looked up into Vic's eyes, and smiled. "Thank you so much, Vic."

He squeezed her hand once before letting go. "Do you need a moment before we go in?" He reached for the door handle.

"If I could just borrow your coat for the next while, I should be fine."

"Anytime." He pulled open the door. She walked into the gym and took in the situation in one glance.

CHAPTER TWENTY-SIX

THINGS WERE NO BETTER THAN before. If possible, they were worse. She took a deep breath and stepped forward. When she could trust her voice, she beckoned to Shana, who stood with a couple of girls huddled around her, all of them with tear-streaked faces.

"Be strong, Shana." Leah gave her friend a smile. Shana bravely smiled back, then raised an eyebrow at Leah's choice of attire. Leah tilted her head at Vic, who moved to where Guy and Javin were wrestling with a couple of boys. They all looked up to him from their position on the ground—the kids with defiance and rebellion, his two teammates with apprehension and despair.

Guy spoke loud enough for Leah to hear him. "It's over, Vic. The top blew off. There has been more swearing and fighting in the last ten minutes than in all previous sessions combined." Leah looked into the despair-filled eyes Guy turned to her. She stared back with determination.

"It's not over yet, Guy. We still have a lot to do. God's not done with these kids yet. We're not going to give up, no matter what." She turned to Javin, and he nodded, a light of hope returning into his eyes.

"What are you going to do now, Leah?" Shana asked, moving her group of girls toward Leah.

Leah hesitated. She could not let her own weakness stand in the way of what must be done. In that moment of decision, she finally realized what Pastor Michael meant by keeping Christ at the center and forefront of whatever they say or do. God must be glorified. Everything must be done in Him, through Him, and for Him.

She inhaled. Despair lost its grip on her. The outcomes of this situation, bleak as they were, were in God's hands. All she had to do was obey and trust Him.

"Boys and girls. Sit in a circle around me on this blue mat." She tapped the blue mattress with her foot. When everyone had made their way to where she stood, she continued.

"We've been working together for ten months now. I understand that many hurtful things were said and done right here a few minutes ago, but before I deal with that, I would like to apologize to all of you. I have forgotten to pray with you before and after each lesson. Let's start doing that now."

Leah knelt down and closed her eyes. "Lord in heaven, thank You for the opportunity to work with these kids. We love each one of them and pray that our teaching and example have been a blessing to their physical and spiritual lives. Today has been a tough day for all of us, Lord. Forgive all the hurtful words that these boys and girls have exchanged. Heal those hearts that have been broken, and restore us back to a loving fellowship even better than what we have enjoyed before. In the name of Jesus, amen."

"Amen." A few of the kids and the rest of Team Set Free chorused.

The door to the gym opened. Leah turned and saw a man that looked very much like the Vault's manager stand in the doorway of the gym. For a few moments, his eyes glowered at her, then focused on the mess around him.

Leah's heart fell.

Vic rose from his seat on the mattress, worked his way toward her, and tapped her shoulder. "Don't worry, Leah. I'll take care of it. Keep doing what you're doing." He gave her a reassuring smile and walked toward the doorway.

The manager turned to Vic and threw his hands toward Leah and the kids, his face furious. His lips moved, but Leah was too far away to hear what he said. She only heard, "Get out of here as soon as possible." And something that sounded too much like, "And don't come back."

Vic replied to him calmly, but Leah couldn't catch what it was he said.

After exchanging a few more words with Vic, the older gentleman spun on his heels and exited Leah's line of vision.

Leah turned, her heart sinking, fearing the worst. She turned to the teens gathered around her and the team and bit her lips. This day was just not turning out well. They were all silent. All looked up to her for direction, some with strange expressions on their faces.

Suddenly, she saw the humor in their situation. She grinned at them. "Y'all must be wondering why I'm wearing Vic's jacket." Nods answered her remark, and several smiles appeared. "Well. Long story short, I was told something was wrong with Vic. The message turned out to be false, and I got a good soaking before I managed to come back. Since I didn't bring a towel or anything, he's been kind enough to lend me his jacket for now." More smiles. Vic returned and went back to his seat, his eyes on Leah. Shana pointed at her hands. Leah nodded. "Yes, I got a few scrapes and bruises along the way. Serves me right for deserting my post." A couple of the boys laughed, and she joined them, relieved that the tension in the room had lessened.

In the back of her mind, she wondered what made her drop everything for Vic. Did she care for him that much? Maybe even *love*? She tore her mind away from the probing thoughts.

"I should not have done that to you all. I'm sorry." She looked at each of her friends and teens by turn.

"We forgive you, Leah," Javin spoke for the group. She returned his smile. *Explain later,* he mouthed silently.

Leah nodded, then turned back to the group. "Your turn, guys. Who could me what happened here?"

Paul raised his hand. "I'll explain. I heard this guy here insult Gina, and I boiled over. Jumped on him. That started the group-wide fight that has just occurred. I'm very sorry I did that. I was trying to protect Gina's dignity." He nodded at Gina, who sat across from him at the other end of the semi-circle around Leah.

"Thank you for apologizing, Paul." Vic nodded to the young man, who'd grown a few inches since he'd first joined them. Vic turned to the fifteen-year-old who had mocked Gina. "What do you have to say to Gina?"

The boy turned to Gina, red-faced. "I'm sorry for what I said to you—I did not mean a word of it." He paused as if unsure of how to go on. "Some random guy told me he would give me ten bucks if I did something that would start a fight or something, and I took the bill." He hung his head. "I knew I shouldn't have done it, but I wanted something pretty bad at the time, and I needed the money . . . "

Leah exchanged glances with Vic and Shana. It had to be Ethan. But would he actually have gone to such lengths? Guy broke the silence after what seemed like minutes. "Buddy, let's talk about that afterward."

The boy nodded without looking up. Gina looked at him, laid a hand on her stomach, and whispered, "I forgive you. I knew you didn't mean it, but it still hurt."

The proud look Paul gave Gina warmed Leah's heart. She turned to Guy, Javin, and Vic and smiled at the boys. "Would you gentlemen mind cleaning up the heavier training equipment? We girls would take care of the foam and other odds and ends."

"As you say, boss." Javin touched his fingers to his forehead in a mock salute, winked, then steered a couple of the teens toward the mess under the monkey bars. Guy nodded, his eyes studying Leah's face for a second before turning to the work at hand.

Vic's face clouded. "Leah, I have something to tell you about later on. About the gym."

"I understand, Vic. Let's get these kids settled, then I'll get Javin to give the parents a call."

Vic nodded, the lines on his forehead receding. He turned to the remaining group of boys and headed over the furthest corner of the gym.

The boys were in good hands. At least for now.

Leah headed over to where Shana was comforting five girls sitting in a circle around her.

Minnie nursed a bruise on her forehead. "How did that happen, Minnie?" Leah crouched beside the teary-eyed girl.

"That other girl began to abuse Gina, verbally. And I stepped in with fists. It turned into an all-out fight between us two. Andrea came into the picture a little later." Her hands left her forehead, her eyes wide with wonderment. "For the first time in my life, I did not care that other kids were laughing at me. I focused only on doing what was right—defending Gina and being a peacemaker. This Parkour stuff really helps." She paused.

"I'm sorry today has been a mess for you and your team, Miss Leah," Andrea said softly. "We all contributed to the mess. Can I take my friends over there and pick up the foam pieces? And, I have to ask a boy to forgive me for calling him a bad name." Andrea's eyes were determined. Leah nodded.

The girls hurried over to join in cleaning up. Talk and laughter soon flowed, though still somewhat strained and awkward. Leah bowed her head and offered a prayer of thanks to the Lord.

Perhaps something good would come out of what has happened. After all, what doesn't kill can only strengthen.

CHAPTER TWENTY-SEVEN

They were holding an impromptu meeting in the front lobby of the Vault. Shana finished briefing the team on exactly what had happened in the gym from beginning to end.

"I thought we lost everything we've been working for this past year." Leah sighed. She leaned back in her chair. Shana had an extra set of clothes in her car, which she had practically forced Leah to change into after their "class" ended for the day.

Shana nodded, contemplative. "When the kids went berserk, I felt like giving up. It was hectic. Vic, you should have been there. We were very near the end of our ropes at that moment."

"Leah left us at the hottest part of the battle," Guy accused, his eyes glaring at Leah.

"I had no idea Ethan would go to such lengths to deceive me," Leah whispered. She looked at her torn hands and sighed.

Javin raised his hand. "I think you owe us the full story, Leah." Shana and Guy nodded in agreement. All waited in anticipation. Leah hesitated, unsure.

"No pressure, Leah. Take your time." Vic patted her shoulder.

Leah took a deep breath and sighed. "All right. Here's the longer version of what I've told you before." She told the team what had happened from the moment she'd stepped out of the gym in answer to the enigmatic text, to the moment she stepped back into the Vault. Leah chose to leave out what happened in the foyer immediately after. One glance at Vic told her he understood.

"I'm so proud of you, Leah." Shana touched her hand, squeezed, and let go. Javin and Guy nodded their approval.

She nodded her thanks to her and looked around at her four friends. Their faces still bore the marks of the tension, pain, and physical struggles they and their boys and girls had just gone through. The fresh memories surfaced once more. Tears began to form in her eyes. What was up with her loss of control over her emotions? She gritted her teeth together, trying not to cry. "I just don't what to do anymore. Everything has crumbled." She swallowed. "I don't know how or if anything could be renewed again."

Vic cleared his throat. "We'll have to pay for the damages caused by the ruckus, or the manager would bar us from ever training here again."

Shana turned to him. "That's what he told you?"

"Yes." Vic nodded. "It's not looking too good."

Shana shifted in her seat, mouth pursed, thoughtful.

Guy stood and paced, his hands in his pockets. His eyes, usually calm and emotionless, were now filled with consternation. "It gets worse. I talked with that boy. The one who said someone paid him to mess everything up. He gave me a description of the man." He stared straight at Leah. "It sounded too much like a description of Ethan."

"And what with the timing of the text and all . . . " Javin nodded, frowning.

"Never liked the looks of the man," Guy grunted in response. Silence greeted his statement.

"What do we do now in light of everything?" Shana finally voiced out the question they were all struggling with.

"We've got Someone greater than all of us combined to look up to and depend on," Vic answered. He looked around at each of the team members. "Let's pray together, then we'll think of what to do as a team with God in the lead."

They knelt, held hands, and bowed their heads.

Even in the midst of all the brokenness, animosity, and unexpected setbacks, they had peace and calm. God was with them. If you have Christ, what more do you need?

After prayers, the team returned to their seats, thoughtful.

"Is there something we could do to give the kids something to work towards as a group?" Shana suggested. "After this ordeal, the kids would probably have a hard time being as cooperative and considerate of each other as they should be or once were."

"Shana has a point. That's a good idea. Maybe hold an event where they could compete . . . no, that defeats the purpose." Guy shrugged, at a loss for ideas

"An anniversary bash where we'd do some shows and fundraising?" Vic suggested.

"Yeah. We'll need something like that. We'll have to use a gym for bad weather days, and the Vault is the best choice we have." Guy leaned forward, his elbows on his knees.

"You're on to something there, Shana." Leah tilted her head in thought. "And I like your idea, Vic. An anniversary bash sounds great, but that would be Canada day. Maybe we could move it to the Saturday of the same week?"

"It's something to think about," Javin shrugged.

Guy agreed. "It sounds like a plausible plan, though. We'll have to get muscle-guy here to think up some elaborate lines and runs for the kids to make the entire thing look more interesting and professional."

Javin jabbed Guy in the ribs, "You're just jealous of my muscles. Grow up."

"Hey. I'm a year older than you," Guy jabbed him back.

"Whatever." Javin laughed at Guy and turned to Leah. "Sounds like a plan. We still have a bit to go, though. I believe I speak for us all when I say today has been a full day, eh?"

They all nodded and rose to leave.

Vic drew her aside. His eyes held hers gently, calmly. "Remember, whatever obstacles you're facing, there's always an opportunity for something better and greater. Like what your shirt says." He smiled.

Leah smiled. She was wearing one of the three shirts Vic had given her for Christmas. The front had a silhouette of a traceur leaping over a wall, and the words "You see a wall. I see a challenge" underneath. On the back, written in splotched gray and a fancy font, was the statement "Every Obstacle is an Opportunity."

"Thanks for all you've done, Vic." She glanced at Vic's coat hung over his arm and chuckled. "It meant a lot to me at the moment."

A beat of silence passed. Vic cleared his throat, shuffled his feet. Leah turned to answer something Javin threw out to her from where Guy, Shana, and himself stood in conversation, and almost missed Vic's quiet question.

"Do you think I could ever be any more than just a friend to you, Leah?"

Leah looked at his face, into his eyes. He simply stared back, allowing her to see if he was sincere or not. She'd wanted to hear those words ever since she'd fallen for him in a child-like fashion in the past, but never thought he'd think of her in any other way than just a childhood friend.

"Do you mean that, Vic?" she whispered.

He nodded, still holding her eyes in his direct gaze. She had to tear her eyes away, for fear of getting lost in them.

She thought back to the things he'd said. The things he'd done for her. The person he'd become.

Had she been that oblivious?

Her heart beat a little faster. She looked up at him again. "You might want to talk to my parents first. If they give you the go-ahead, I don't see why not."

His smile was wide and contagious, and he gave her hand a quick squeeze. "Praise the Lord," he whispered. "You have no idea how happy that makes me." He stepped back, eyes shining. "I'll give your parents a call as soon as possible."

Leah smiled at him, her heart fit to burst with joy and thankfulness. Every dark cloud, every hard day wasn't without its own joys and blessings. Her face clouded for a few seconds as her mind went to the problems and difficulties Team Set Free and their teens were facing.

Vic caught her expression, touched her chin, and made eye contact with her. His voice was serious but joyful and strong. "Everything is going to be all right, Leah. God is with us."

Leah nodded. "Amen."

CHAPTER TWENTY-EIGHT

LATE MAY . . .

"Kids, we have an idea." Shana stood in front of the twelve teens assembled in the main gym inside the Vault. The young adults' faces glowed with excitement as Shana outlined the details of the anniversary day bash. "We're going to hold the show in this gym. All of you would go in teams of two—some of you are going to work primarily on bars, others with vaults, yet others with flips and whatnot. Between now and July first, we are going to work out the schedule and specific moves each of you are going to perform. That's five weeks total, between then and now."

A few of the girls covered their mouths, excited smiles stretching across their lips.

"We'll let you guys know the nitty-gritty details once we've got all the basic things nailed down. But for today, that's all you need to know. Let's get started!"

The kids separated. Leah was in charge of coordinating and organizing each of the four teams Guy, Vic, Jav, and Shana were leading. She made her way over to where Shana guided Minnie and Andrea into a complicated line.

The two girls worked on a complementary duet of precisions and vaults, and Shana choreographed their flips to happen simultaneously, spinning in opposite directions away from each other.

"That's it." Minnie and Andrea beamed at Shana from their perch on two plastic obstacles. Shana flashed a smile at them and continued, turning to Leah. "We're going to put the moves in time to music, but first we're going to run through this whole thing two more times to make sure you've got this down pat. We've got other things to work on after this."

"Aww . . . " The girls whined, smiling. They loved it.

Vic waved Leah over, then explained how two other girls would be doing vaults over various obstacles. The girls ran through their personalized line once, then beamed with pride. Leah clapped for them and called out words of encouragement.

Leah smiled to herself, then walked over to where Guy and Javin were working with the four boys.

Guy looked down from his crouched position on top of a steel bar, critiquing and making sure that Paul and Owen were properly doing their bar laches. "Leah, I think these boys are ready to fine-tune their moves."

"Doing what?"

"Each of these boys would do something different on these bars, all with the idea of getting around, through, and under this huge complex with the most creative movement they could think of."

He called Paul over. "Paul, go through your line again. Focus on having a loose yet firm grip on the bars, and landing lightly but solidly on the bar as you swing upwards to a standing position."

Paul nodded, jumped onto the bar in front of him, and began to swing from bar to bar. He swung himself twice, then threw a backflip into the space between two bars, landing on the bar underneath him with his flexed knees. In that upside-down position, he reached for the bar he was hanging from, hung with his arms between his knees, moved his two feet to where his knees were just now, and swung to a standing position on top of the bar. He stood and bowed. Leah clapped.

Paul was not finished yet. He leaped into the air, grabbed the bar directly above him with one hand, and then swung from one bar to another.

"They're going to be the team to primarily perform on the bars, eh?" Leah called out to Guy.

Guy looked at her, his attention diverted for a while from the boy in the bars below him, who came nearer and nearer to where Guy crouched. "That's Paul and Owen's area of expertise, I think. What . . . "

Paul had reached the bar Guy was on and chucked one of Guy's feet off the bar with a raised fist, grinning wide.

Instinctively, Guy reached forward to steady himself: but there was nothing for him to hold on. He teetered on the bar, leaning too far back to catch himself upright. Leah saw him swivel his head around, trying to gauge the quickest way to regain his balance and dignity. His eyes latched onto the side of the poles holding the structure of bars up below him. He allowed himself to fall, twisted around in mid-air, and grabbed onto a vertical bar. He tightened his abs, straightening out his legs into a human flag.

After holding the position for five seconds, Guy dropped onto the floor and jogged over to Leah. "These boys are ready to move on to the group demonstration if the other kids are ready."

"That's great news. The rest of them will be ready in a few minutes. Let's jump and flip some more."

CHAPTER TWENTY-NINE

THE CHAIRS FILLED HALF OF the gym. There was also a viewing balcony, eight feet above the bottom of the two-storey-high Parkour gym. The other half of the gym was filled with Parkour equipment—bar structures, plastic obstacles of all sizes and heights, and a center stage where a single microphone stood on a make-shift stage in the center of all the Parkour training objects.

Leah wandered around in the foyer outside the gym, encouraging the twelve young Parkour traceurs who would be performing today. She tied the girls' hair and checked to make sure that all shoelaces were tucked inside the shoes to prevent trips.

"You all know what you're doing, right?" Leah spoke to the group at large. A few of the boys nodded at her. Minnie's eyes widened as she shook her head just the tiniest bit. "You'll do just fine, Minnie. Shana would be making sure that . . . "

"Shana?" Where did she go?

The girl in question suddenly rounded the corner behind a fast-walking Vic, who glanced at Leah with an amused smile.

"Sorry, I've been detained by . . . " He gestured at Shana, who shot Leah a mischievous grin that matched the one on Vic's face. He winked at her and sauntered over to the side door of the gym. "Kids, are we all ready?" he said in a stage whisper.

"Yes!" the teens chorused. Leah thought she heard Minnie squeal.

"We're going to present our testimonies and stories after the show, eh?" Paul tapped Leah's arm, tilting his head to her.

"Yes." Leah nodded, her heart alive with joy.

"My mother and father came together today." Owen took Andrea's hand in his and squeezed. "There's been talk of them getting together again, and our family has been working together to make life easier for all of us. Would you mind if my sister and I went up to say something as well?"

"That would be wonderful. You guys could go after Paul. Then Gina and Minnie would go after you guys. And then we'll have the final big show."

"All set?" Vic smiled even wider at them, then ushered the kids in behind a bunch of the larger plastic obstacles. "Stay here until we call you guys out. You know the drill." They all nodded with excitement. "All right. Leah. You're coming with me." He held out a hand.

Leah looked at him in surprise. "This was not what we did during the rehearsal."

"Trust me." He flashed her a calm, happy smile, grabbed her unwilling hand, and hauled her to the front stage.

"It's all yours, bro," Javin handed the mic to Vic, raised an eyebrow when he saw Leah, and raised both when he saw Leah's hand still trapped in Vic's. Then he smiled knowingly at her and went to the back of the gym.

Vic lifted the mic to his mouth. "Ladies and gentlemen. Exactly one year ago, this young woman who I'm holding by the hand had a vision. It is one so grand and so unbelievable that only in the past few weeks have we realized just how great an opportunity God has blessed us with. And without further ado, I'll let our boss speak for herself." He handed her the mic, laughter in his eyes.

"You . . . " She had no words. She shook her head at him, helpless. He laughed and headed back to the kids near the back of the stage.

Leah turned to face the assembled people—young and old. She saw her family seated in the audience, waving at her.

"Thank you all for coming. My name is Leah Jung, and I am a Parkour athlete who's been training for a few years. A year ago, I was given a vision to form a team that would bring this sport to young people who need to be set free from fears, doubts, and self-perceived disabilities. Team Set Free, as I call your name, please step out of the shadows. Our one and only, Guy Raymond."

Guy swung off a bar behind her to her right and threw a double front flip, landing neatly beside Leah. He waved to the audience, then stepped back.

"Javin Trevor." Jav ran up, did a few front handsprings in a row, and snatched Leah's microphone. "Shana Quinones, who has just agreed to be my girlfriend."

Shana kong-vaulted her way over an obstacle to stand beside Javin. "Did you have to tell them all that just like that?"

"Why not?"

Leah plucked the mic from him. "And last but not least, the guy that introduced me to you all . . . Victor Menchaca."

Vic stepped on stage, waving at the audience.

"These four friends have stood by me through thick and thin. When I broke down, they encouraged me. When I was weak, they were strong."

"We could say the same of you, boss," Javin interjected, to the chuckles of a few in the audience.

"Our vision and goal was to change the lives of all we work with, and to show them the power and awesomeness of God through this sport. As you get to meet the kids who have been with us for the past year, you'll see that God *has* been working in their lives. We give Him all the glory. We could do nothing without Him—we could have done nothing for Him but by His Grace and saving strength."

Leah handed to mic back to Shana, who took the role of emcee for the shows. The rest of the team stepped off the stage and stood to the side.

"Let's have our girls come out and show us flips and precisions."

Minnie and Andrea hopped out from behind two different blocks and began to perform precision jumps from obstacle to obstacle, jumping and flipping in time to the music. With their faces alight with smiles and their braids and ponytails flying, the girls were alive with joyful movement. After a few minutes, they stood together, linked hands, and bowed to the audience. Leah's eyes watered. She clapped just as hard as she could.

The boys were next. It was truly all coming together.

"And now you're in for a treat. Members from Team Set Free will put on their own special show for your enjoyment. Please leave your applause until the end—that is, until we bow," Shana smiled and stepped back from the mic, winking at Leah.

Laughter swept over the audience, then a hush of anticipation settled in. Leah watched as Guy and Javin entered the stage from two different sides of the gym, their eyes intent on Shana, who stood with her back to the audience, hands on her hips.

Apparently, this was a drama type of show. Guy and Jav acted the part of two young men who happened to fall in love with the same girl, Shana. They danced around her, throwing moves, trying to impress her and outdo each other at the same time. Guy incorporated hilarious facial expressions as he swung, and jumped, and flipped over, under, and around the different obstacles in front of Shana, while Javin made ridiculous noises to match the intensity and difficulty of his moves—much like how little boys would mimic the sound of trucks and motorcycles when playing with plastic toy figurines. The three of them had the audience in stitches by the time Javin threw himself, breathless, at Shana's feet, and Guy looked on dejectedly as Shana raised Jav to his knees and offered him her hand. Javin and Shana bowed and took their leave. The audience hooted and applauded.

Then it was time for her run—with Vic.

Vic held out a hand to her, and she stood up, got on stage with him, and held his hand with a smile. He motioned for her to jump onto his back, held out his arms upwards, and she climbed onto his shoulders, standing up and reaching for the highest bars above her.

They began to move in tandem to the music, timing the flips and moves to match the beats of the song. She could not hold in the smile as she felt the music pulsating through her, her body doing what she loved. Overcoming obstacles using only the body and mind. And she did. When God showed her a way to glorify her and help those in need of healing in the community, she'd overcome the obstacles and problems to realize the vision He'd given her.

It was a promise she'd made—a promise of love for others, for God, her friends, her kids, her team, herself.

She was about to kick and swing herself into a bar lache when she noticed Vic's form flying in the air towards her. Vic swung and landed onto the bar she was hanging from, their hands touching at the bar, their faces less than two inches apart.

Their eyes locked for a second, their faces inches apart. Vic just smiled. Leah grinned back at him.

Vic whispered, "We're not finished yet. I'll get us swinging, then you'll flip back, and I'll flip back from my side. Land standing on the bars below."

"This was not in the rehearsal," Leah muttered. He'd already started swinging both of them.

"One, two, three." Vic mouthed, then his hands flew off. Hers came off the next split second, and her body turned two full rotations in the air.

Leah landed on a bar and balanced. She jumped off the bar and joined Vic on the ground, grinning as wide as she could.

The song melted away, and Vic reached for her hand, leading her to the stage and initiating a bow. The audience clapped. Vic walked to the mic and let go of Leah's hand.

"Thanks for watching and encouraging us with your applause. Now we'd like to invite a few of the kids who've been with us to come up and share their stories with you. Sit tight."

Vic led Leah off the stage and took a seat beside her.

Paul walked out from the corner of the gym and up to the microphone.

He smiled at the audience, his face creasing. "Hello. My name is Paul. Two years ago, I had my life all planned out. I was going to live my dream of being a fulltime athlete, specializing in marathons and triathlons. Then an accident crushed them all," he described what had happened. "I was crushed. I had no hope. The one thing in my life that brought me joy was taken from me. I slipped into depression and began to withdraw from friends and family. On top of that, I had a hard time forgiving the person who forgot to close the car door and led me to where I was a year ago. Broken and hopeless.

"Then, one day mom was reading the newspaper and came across an ad about a team of Parkour people. The team was going to train young people to overcome obstacles, mental and physical. Mom asked if I wanted to go, and I said 'Sure.' That in itself was a big step in the right direction. It was the first time I initiated anything in over a year.

"I came to the opening party, hoping to find something to take away some of the hurt and disappointment I've been carrying around for a long time. It ended up being so much more than that. I've seen these guys and girls—I mean the team, but they're not that much older than me anyways—help each other, forgive each other, hold each other up. That was the first step toward finding peace with the burden of blame and suffering I've been unable, and unwilling, to let go of.

"Doing Parkour . . . my mom was skeptical. The sport looked so dangerous, so active, so risky. But over time, as I grew stronger and more confident—less like the shadow of myself I was before I joined them—she started to be happy for me, started to stand beside me and cheer me on.

"You see me up here today. I've done things I never thought I'd be able to do, much less do painlessly. After my accident, I thought my life as I'd known it, was over. Team Set Free has shown me that once

I got rid of that crippling mindset, I could, step by step, overcome obstacles and boundaries that aren't really that hard to overcome after all. I've learned to face life head on and not blame my suffering and setbacks on other people, to take things seriously and enjoy movement again. I probably will not be able to get back into competitive sports, but this I know, I won't be afraid to reach for ever greater heights."

The audience broke into applause. Paul paused and gripped the microphone. "Clap for God, people. He made all this possible. It was this group, this team, that brought me to the knowledge of God and the change he could make in a person's life. I know they're not perfect. I've seen them slip. But they've guided me to the truth through their example, dedication, and love to us, to God, and to each other. And for that, I am forever grateful." His voice choked. "Thank you, Team Set Free, for giving me back my life a hundred fold."

Leah sniffed. Tears dimmed her eyes as the almost-fully grown young man walked off the stage with his head held high, eyes shining. She dabbed at her tears.

Vic's hand closed over her and squeezed. "God is wonderful, is He not?" He whispered to her. Leah could only nod, her heart full.

Owen and Andrea stood up. "Mom and Dad, you guys come over, too," Owen ordered, walking to the front of the stage. A few laughed as the surprised middle-aged couple went on stage. Owen grabbed the mic.

"My name is Owen, and this is my family—my dad, my sister, and my mom. A year ago, we were fighting each other. We could barely talk without arguing or yelling at each other. Andrea would shove me, I'd call her names I'm ashamed to repeat now, and I'd push her back.

That's one reason why she's so strong now: I'm this much bigger than she is."

Andrea stepped up and took the mic. "But more than that, I have to tell you about something that could be explained only as a miracle. Once the team knew that our father and mother were getting divorced, they told us they were going to pray for us, and they encouraged us to pray for them, too. That got us thinking about God, and prayer, and things like that. Mom? You want to talk about it?"

"Okay," the woman reached and spoke into the mic hesitantly. "A year ago, I'd given up all hope on our marriage. I had been a professed Christian before, but over the years my faith had wavered and finally snuffed out under stress and simple day-to-day life. My husband and I fought daily over anything and everything. You married men and women out there would know, we were at a breaking point.

"Then one day, Andrea walked up to me and asked why I did not read the bible to them anymore. Why had I stopped praying with them at night? I remembered doing those things when they were toddlers, but that was so long ago.

"But those simple questions gave me hope that perhaps our family could be brought together again."

Owen picked up the mic, "We prayed hard. The team prayed, too. I know this is not as related to Parkour as Paul's speech, but I just want to get this out. It took an awful lot of courage and determination to just share with our parents how we felt about their decision to divorce, about why we'd stopped going to church, about what was wrong with our family—it was hard. Every time we talked, we fought.

"But learning to do Parkour here, with this team, I've gotten my resolve and mental stamina trained. If the thing needed to be done, we had to do it, no matter how many tries it took, no matter how long it took for me to learn that one move. I was able to transition that thinking and perseverance in to my daily life."

"On top of that, for me, it was the ability to overcome my fear," Andrea spoke now, her voice carrying through the gym. "I had to face many difficult jumps and passes, knowing that if I missed, I'd fall. I might get hurt. But I had to do it. That helped me face challenges in my life and our family life with more confidence and positivity than I ever imagined I could have."

"And that's all I have to say for now. Thanks for listening."

"Oh, and by the way, we're the Wannabe family!"

The audience laughed and clapped, thinking it was a joke. The reunited family left the stage, holding hands.

Leah squeezed Vic's hand, too touched for words.

Next was Minnie. She reached up for the mic, unhooked it from the stand, and held it in front of her.

"My name is Minnie. When I came to Team Set Free, I was a nervous, self-conscious wreck. I was worried about everything—but mostly about how others saw me. They would laugh at how fat I was, the colors I wore, my clothing choices, the way I did certain things. You get the idea. It got so bad that I was hurting myself by not doing anything that I was just the slightest bit concerned I would not do perfectly or especially well. I was afraid. My mother feared that I was teetering at the edge of a nervous breakdown.

"As a last resort, she signed me up to this Parkour training thing, maybe hoping that the interesting exercise would get me to lose a few pounds. Thankfully, I have, as you can see. My clothes are starting to fit me better.

"But what a year it had been. Training Parkour and learning to do things like flip upside down, and jump from ledge to ledge, has taught me to live and move without being afraid of what others might think of me. Say if I wanted to, or had to, do a flip in the air, and I was afraid that my shirt would lift, then I would never be able to do the flip. I had to focus on what I was doing and forget about what I feared others would say or think about. I remember our first lesson. Leah told me that I can't control what other people think of me: what I could control, however, is to do my best at whatever I am doing.

"I don't have much to say, other than this: I'm so thankful that my mother signed me up to join Team Set Free. They have helped me shed the shackles of self-doubt, self-consciousness, and the deceptive self-esteem that were all part of my pride and ego. In this sport, your ego spells your death. You must push yourself, do what you can, and keep improving, no matter if people think you're crazy, or too fat, or a little . . . touched in the head. I am now set free from the life I had been living before. Thank you."

She handed to mic to Gina, who shyly smiled at the clapping audience and bowed her head for a moment. Then she lifted her head and gazed bravely into the audience.

"One year ago, I would not have thought I would be able to do what I am doing now—to stand on a stage and talk to family, friends, and strangers. Before joining Team Set Free, I was painfully shy. I've even seen doctors who could not understand why I would hyperventilate and blank out every time I had to do something in front of more than two people.

"I've been teased and laughed at a lot—for my height, for my grades, for my accent. Anything. It did not bother me as much as they did my friend Minnie, but I channeled my hurt into distancing myself from everyone. To interact as little as possible, to keep myself safe.

"I have been scared and shy since I was three years old, but when my nervous symptom increased, my life became a mess.

"Until I came to Team Set Free. They showed me, through this sport, that I could do more than what I thought was possible. That I had to be confident in doing what I knew I could do. That I needed to practice what I could improve and learn what I still do not know. This sport has taught me so much about being able to enjoy what I do, no matter how many people are watching me. I had to focus on what I was doing in order to make the jump. Hyperventilation was not an option. I mean, if I did, I would be too stiff and tense to do any of the tricks you saw me do earlier.

"I want to thank Team Set Free for bringing me out of the prison I'd been building for myself ever since I started high school. Now I can greet life, and the people I meet on this road, with confidence. Thank you. And thank You, God."

She replaced the mic and curtsied to the audience, then skipped off stage.

Leah got up from her seat, motioned for Vic to join her on stage, then picked up the mic.

"Now ladies and gentlemen—for the last show of the day. The entire team and all the kids who are present with us today would give you a final encore demonstration of Parkour—joy and freedom in motion."

Shana, Guy, and Javin walked out from behind a stack of obstacles, the twelves teens right behind them.

They linked hands in a long line and bowed to the audience.

They waited. The opening notes of their team's "theme song" were played, and one by one, the team members and kids left the front of the stage to run, jump, and play on the various obstacles behind them, freestyle.

Leah turned, took Shana's hand, smiled, and together they performed a series of flips, hands linked.

Then they joined the smiling kids and team on the bars and blocks, as the fitting words of the song drifted through the gym. The lyrics spoke of regrets, a less-than-happy past. How things could have been different, could have been better. How all was to be laid at the foot of the cross, how each of us were to live as set apart children of God. How our past and present experiences—good or bad—were all coming together to shape who we were meant to be.

Scars were scars. For the kids around her, for each of them, the years in the past and the years before them would not be all roses and sunshine. There would be obstacles. There would be trials. They'd spent the past trying to get out of them, trying to live free from fears and disabilities.

Now they had learned to overcome obstacles of the physical kind. And in doing so, they have forced themselves to break through fears, break through doubts, to see reality as it is, face it down, and deal with it.

Even on something as unforgiving as concrete.

Leah swung on top of the highest bar and took a breather, looking down at her friend and team members, at the teens she'd stood with and worked with, interacting with one another, freerunning, with smiles on their faces. Joy in motion.

The team had come full circle. The teens had truly been set free.

EPILOGUE

THE TEAM GATHERED IN THE park a week after the anniversary party. They sat side by side on the concrete wall—Guy, Vic, Leah, Shana, and Javin, in that order.

"God has surpassed all our expectations, hasn't He?" Shana sipped from her water bottle, her eyes traveling from one friend to another.

"He has. Beyond just this vision." Leah nodded, looking into Shana's eyes. "I never told you guys this before, but when I ran back to the Vault on that day . . . I overcame the biggest personal obstacle I had." Guy tilted his head and stared at her, curious. Leah smiled. "A kong-gainer. I broke my knee going over the wall years ago, and never touched that move again. When Ethan tried to hold me back from getting back to our kids, I just kept running and jumping away from him toward the Vault." Leah smiled to herself. "And before I knew it, I'd thrown a kong-gainer over a wall in my way."

"Having a goal or purpose that overwhelms all fear and doubt and spurs you to action tends to do that." Vic looked at her, pride in his eyes. "I'm glad that obstacle is passed for you."

Leah looked out over the sunset. "You're right. I'm thankful for that."

Silence reigned for a few minutes.

Leah fingered the loose pebbles on the wall. Tiny stones. Just like those pebbles she'd brushed off the wall that fateful day years ago. Small, sharp, insignificant. Just like each of them. But now the sharpness was their power, their impact. The hardness was their perseverance, their determination to go on despite all odds. Their small size a symbol of each human being, small and insignificant.

But together, they could do so much. For God.

Vic reached his arm around her shoulders and squeezed. Leah touched the engagement ring on her finger and smiled gently at Vic.

"I've never thanked you for bringing Shana and me together, boss." Javin interposed, his eyes shining.

"It wasn't me. It was the Lord. And all of you." She smiled at her friends, joy and thankfulness overflowing in her heart.

The sun was setting over the horizon. Guy was silent, his eyes looking out into the sky, beyond the city line. He turned to her after a while. "I thought you were crazy with this idea at first, Leah. But look at what an impact this sport has made on the kids who've been working with us."

Leah bowed her head. "I know. It was a radical idea, and Parkour cannot help everyone. But for the few whose lives could be changed by this—past, present, and future—we will continue on."

"It's a worthy cause. We're standing right beside you, Leah." Javin intoned soberly, his arm around Shana's shoulders. "The world's our playground, and the earth is ripe for harvest."

"But the laborers are few. And Parkour cannot help everyone the same way it has helped the kids who've been with us." Vic said. Guy nodded, silent.

Shana swept her arm over the cityscape. "There are many who are in need of Christ, who so desperately need to be set free."

There was a moment of silence as the team faced the setting sun, their faces hardening with resolve.

Finally, Leah spoke.

"We go to them. Each life counts. And we will do all we can to lead them to the One who can set them free."

RECOMMENDED RESOURCES ON PARKOUR AND FREERUNNING

BOOKS:

- *Breaking the Jump* by Julie Angel—This book documents the story of how Parkour came to be what it is today.

- *Parkour Roadmap* by Max Henry—I have personally found this book to be one of the most helpful books on the market for both information on Parkour, and detailed instructions on how to perform basic moves. The list of resources at the end of this book—much longer than this one, I must say—is invaluable, especially for those just starting out.

- *Parkour Strength Training: Overcome Obstacles for Fun and Fitness* by Ryan Ford—This is the book to go when looking for direction and advice on how to condition yourself before, during, and after you train. Being strong and flexible before attempting tricks lowers risk of injury significantly: I definitely recommend getting a copy of this book!

- *The Natural Method* by Georges Hebert—Originally written in French, there is a great translation by Philippe Til that could be found on Amazon.com. I highly recommend that you read the thoughts and philosophy of this forefather of Parkour.

This book helped me to understand and incorporate some of Parkour's foundational moves and mindset.

VIDEOS:

- *Generation Yamasaki: A Documentary*—This is the story of the Yamasaki, a group of French kids who gave birth to this amazing sport known as Parkour today. This is the real story behind the movie Yamasaki, told by the athletes themselves. Generation Yamasaki has been one of the most inspiring and informative videos I've watched regarding Parkour.

- *Learn Parkour & Freerunning: Ultimate Tutorial for Beginners* by Jason Paul—This video touches on the most foundational moves of Parkour/freerunning. There are hundreds, probably even thousands, of tutorials and videos out there, but this is one of the best videos out there with which to get started, in my opinion. It is a great introduction to parkour, training, and how to perform specific movements. Check it out!

For more information about
Odelia Chan
and
Obstacles
please visit:

www.odeliachan.com

For more information about
AMBASSADOR INTERNATIONAL
please visit:

www.ambassador-international.com

Thank you for reading this book. Please consider leaving us a review on your social media, favorite retailer's website, Goodreads or Bookbub, or our website.

More from Ambassador International

Determined to survive, an orphaned Esther must fight a rising new order in a broken America. This new order, the Federation of Acceptance, enforces directives that jeopardize human rights and beliefs. Esther must decide where she stands as she faces disappearing teachers, murdered classmates, and a traitorous ex-flame, and be forced to make decisions that will affect the lives of everyone around her.

Caleb Sawyer crosses paths with Ellie Thompson, the mysteriously difficult new girl in town. His obsession with her leads them both on an adventure full of opportunities and challenges. When the unthinkable happens, his faith is put to the test. Caleb's faith comes full circle, and he learns that God is good, and that he truly does have a future and a hope.

Johann Smedley Oberhausen is a 16-year-old child prodigy with gifts in academics and baseball, but when he and his friends in the Eleutheria Club record top-secret phone calls from two devious, powerful men, Johann is forced to take a break from his college classes to help stop an impending world disaster.

www.ingramcontent.com/pod-product-compliance
Lightning Source LLC
Chambersburg PA
CBHW071431260626
47170CB00008B/2667